DEAD BALL

Michael Balkind

SterlingHouse Publisher, Inc. Pittsburgh, PA

DEAD BALL

Perothrillers

ISBN-10: 1-56315-453-6
ISBN-13: 978-1-56-315453-9
Trade Paperback

Library of Congress #2009922439

Requests for information should be addressed to:
SterlingHouse Publisher, Inc.
3468 Babcock Boulevard
Pittsburgh, PA 15237
info@sterlinghousepublisher.com
www.sterlinghousepublisher.com

Pero Thrillers
is an imprint of SterlingHouse Publisher, Inc.

Cover Design: Brandon M. Bittner
Interior Design: Kathleen M. Gall

Printed in U.S.A.

Dedication

I dedicate this novel to my father,
ROBERT,
my sister,
BETSY
and my grandmother,
HELEN.
The three of you may be gone
but you'll always be loved and never forgotten.

Thanks

As always, I want to thank my wife and kids
for putting up with me
as I follow my creative passions and dreams.
GREER, BETSY, HUNTER and REID,
I love you all so much.

1

The four-seat golf cart skidded to an abrupt stop, launching the Secret Service agent in the passenger seat into the windshield. The agent who had been driving jumped out and darted into the pristine gardens bordering the basketball arena.

Until that moment, the tour of the AllSport athletic center had been similar to every other, except today, the person sitting in the golf cart next to golf legend, Reid Clark, happened to be the President of the United States. The First Lady, along with another agent, was in the back seat. As usual, comments of amazement about the facility and athletes in training had flowed non-stop from the honored guests. Reid's cart was boxed inside four full carts of agents. An additional cart of agents was ahead of them and another behind.

Reid saw the head cart stop but was far enough back that he had no idea what the commotion was all about. He heard multiple agents' radios beep and tried to listen to the quick commands. Suddenly the carts on both sides pulled close and the agent in Reid's cart commanded him to stop. Agents immediately surrounded his cart with guns drawn. Out of nowhere appeared a black Suburban that skidded to a halt only yards away. The President and First Lady were whisked into the truck. The heavy reinforced doors slammed shut and the truck sped off, tires spinning, kicking up a spray of dirt and grass. Before he had left, the President made sure that four agents remained with Reid.

Reid still had no idea what the problem was. With intense curiosity he drove toward the group of agents at the site of the problem. AllSport security guards had also begun to appear. An agent yelled for Reid to stop, but he paid the agent no heed. It was not like Reid to take orders from anyone, especially on his own turf. He wanted to know what had happened, and no one was going stop him. He pulled up next to the other carts and walked past the group of agents standing by the garden. He saw an arm protruding from under a bush and pushed his way through the surrounding men. Looking at the body, his heart skipped a beat. His gasp was loud and tears immediately welled up in his eyes. Lying there with a bullet hole in his left temple and blood covering his face was Bob Thomas, Reid's dearest friend and the Chief Financial Officer of The Inner City Sports Foundation and AllSport.

Reid's eyes fluttered and he became light-headed. He needed to sit down before he collapsed. *Too late*. Two of the agents closest to him caught him as he crumpled to the ground. They gave him a moment to revive, and then helped him to his cart and drove him to the administration building, where he had his office. Art Fornham, AllSport's director, met them in Reid's office after being informed of the situation.

Nancy Baron, Reid's assistant, left his side just as Art walked in. As she turned, her long, wavy, auburn hair brushed Art's arm. Reid noticed as Art turned to admire her nicely curved, tight, athletic body. Nancy was a common topic of conversation for many of the male athletes on campus. Her husband, John Baron, an NFL quarterback, regularly helped train athletes at AllSport. Seeing Nancy pull a tissue from her pocket and wipe her eyes as she left, made Reid appreciate her attempt at consoling him. She was obviously emotionally distraught also.

Art, a fit, middle-aged man with short grayish-white hair, walked over, took a seat on the couch next to Reid and quietly said, "Buck and Jay are already on the way in Chopper 2. The local Chief of Police and his detectives will be here shortly. Reid, I'm so sorry. I know how close you were with Bob. I just don't get it. Who the hell would want to kill him? AllSport's security has been at level four ever since..., well, you know. Dammit, this is terrible. We can't close down again."

With a pained expression, Reid said, "Take it easy, Art, we'll figure out what to do together. As soon as everyone's here we'll have a meeting. I want all of Bob's staff prepared to stay late tonight. They each need to be interviewed. We need to inform them about this before rumors start to fly around the camp. You and I should go speak to them together. Might as well do it now."

"Yeah, I guess," Art sighed. "Are you sure you're up to it?"

"No, I'm not sure, but we really don't have a choice, do we?"

"I guess not."

The accounting staff was small for a foundation with such a large cash flow. Although companies the same size as ICSF have accounting departments of over fifty people, Bob kept his staff small in order to prevent greed from becoming an issue. Millions of dollars were donated weekly to the foundation, and that kind of money could be very tempting to the wrong people. Bob hand-selected his staff of 25 from various companies that he had either worked for or with in the past. They were a very tight group, like a family, with Bob acting more as mentor than boss to all.

Reid and Art knew this would be a difficult, tear-filled meeting. They exited the elevator on the second floor and walked down the burgundy carpeted hallway to the accounting office. Entering the stark, bright bullpen of cubicles, it was obvious that no one had heard the tragic news yet. Twenty people were going through their daily business of making sure that the boatloads of money that flowed in and out of their hands were accounted for to the last penny.

Stressed but happy faces greeted Reid and Art as they walked into the room. Reid nodded to a few of the employees as he walked to an area where he could address the entire staff.

"May I have everyone's attention please? Could you all stop whatever you're doing and join us?" He waited for the employees to gather round, then took a deep breath to calm his nerves. "I don't know how else to say this, so I'm just going to be direct. Your boss and my best friend, Bob Thomas, was found dead on campus a little while ago." Moans, cries and loud gasps filled the room. Wiping a tear from his cheek, Reid continued. "It appears he was murdered. We don't have any more information at the moment, but Jay Scott and the local police will be here shortly. I know this is going to be difficult for all of you. Believe me it's hard for me too, but we are going to need everyone's cooperation. I would appreciate it if you would all stick around until Jay's team has had a chance to speak with each of you. I know many of you have a long commute; we will make rooms available for you in the guest buildings. I will also have our camp psychologist available for anyone who needs to talk. For that matter, my door will be open as well." Tears once again welled up in Reid's eyes. "Once funeral arrangements have been made and we know a little more, we will allow for rotating time off for all of you. Until then, please just do your best to keep everything in this department running as smoothly as possible." Reid looked around the room. "Does anyone know where Joe Spinelli is?"

"He's on vacation in Nepal," said Art. "He's not due back for a week. He's actually climbing Everest. I guess we need to try to contact him and cut his vacation short. He'll just have to understand, and we'll make it up to him somehow."

Joe Spinelli, the director of the accounting department, pretty much ran the show. He had worked under Bob in two previous jobs and was like a walking computer. He crunched numbers faster without a calculator than most people could with one.

"Until Joe comes back, Lisa Difillipi is in charge," said Reid. "That is, of course, if you're OK with it, Lisa."

"You can count on me," Lisa said in a sullen fashion. Lisa Difillipi was the head of the largest accounting area: Charitable Contribution Revenue, or CCR. She was also very close with Bob, as everyone knew.

"You all know where to find us if you need us," said Reid. "Try to keep it together, folks. We have complete faith in you," he said as he and Art left the office.

As they rode the elevator back up to the executive offices on the fifth floor, Reid said, "I need to call Bob's wife. I should go tell her in person, but I can't leave. I'll get Shane to go spend the night with her." He sighed, thinking of his beautiful wife. "Oh, Art, I can't believe he's dead." Reid's head was hung low. He then said with venom in his voice, "I'm going to get whoever did this, if it's the last thing I do."

Just then Art's two-way radio beeped and he held it up to his mouth. "Come in."

"Hey, boss, Dave Wheeler, the Chief of Police is here with a few detectives, and they're heading over to the crime scene," said Alan Fox, AllSport's Director of Security.

"Thanks, Alan, but I'm not ready to talk to them yet," Art said. "I'll head over in a little while with Buck and Jay. Al, when they land, please come up to the boardroom with them."

"You got it. Hey, Art, you and Reid should know that word of this is traveling fast all over campus."

Art sighed. "I guess that's to be expected. Let your team know they have to keep everybody calm and away from the scene. If there is any trouble, let us know immediately."

"Roger that. See you in a while. By the way, how's Reid doing?"

"I don't think it's really hit him yet. He's been too busy so far, but he's about to call Bob's wife. That won't be easy."

2

It had been almost two years since the attempt on Reid's life, and although he was a strong individual, physically and emotionally he never completely got over the incident. Reid was an exceptional person. Despite the shock of the botched assassination attempt, he had maintained his position at the top of the Professional Golf Association's leader board longer than any golfer in history. He had become a golf icon within the past few years. He was admired by the entire nation both on the golf course and off. Kids of all ages looked up to him and aspired to follow in his shoes. Men cheered him on with a sort of jealous admiration. His rugged good looks and athletic build mesmerized women. Everyone respected his philanthropic endeavors, especially The Inner City Sports Foundation, or ICSF.

The Foundation and its training camp, AllSport, had become one-of-a-kind institutions. ICSF gave underprivileged kids with professional potential in just about any sport the training to become champions. Many of the chosen kids would have ended up in jail or worse if not for the ICSF. After four years, the results of the ICSF were already changing the level of competition in American sports. It was thought that, with another few years of ICSF training, American contestants would dominate the Olympics, both winter and summer. It amazed people that the athletes they were watching on TV might never have made it to the field, court, ring or wherever they played their sport, if not for ICSF. No other facility in the world provided training in as many sports as AllSport. Athletes trained and competed in practically every sport you could name. It had become uncommon to watch a professional sporting event without seeing an athlete who had been trained at AllSport.

Reid had added a new division recently. It was given the task of creating new sports. The Director of the division, John Klien, was given an open budget and his own arena. Everything about the division was highly secret. The staff, mostly athletes and engineers, was sworn to secrecy and all signed non-disclosure contracts. Pros from different sports were brought in as consultants depending on the type of sport that was in the works. To name the division, Reid held a camp-wide contest. Names of all types were entered: NewSport, Create-a-sport, Invent-a-sport, Sports Design, and The Sport Incubator, to name a few. The chosen name, NewSport, became nationally recognized within months. Contests were held that brought in innovative ideas from all over the country. Hundreds of emails with new concepts were received every month. While some were interesting, most were bizarre. The prizes for the creators of the chosen ideas were invitations to AllSport to help with development.

In the few years since inception, the ICSF and AllSport had become the foremost charity and sports training facility in the world. In fact, there was nothing even close. In the beginning, when Reid and his agent, Morty (Buck) Green, started the Foundation, the concept alone brought in donations of such tremendous proportions that the Board of Directors often laughed at the rapidly increasing size of the bank account. They searched for kids with talent. When they found the right ones they often had to ask the pros who trained them to use their team's professional training facilities. Money was spent on recruiting, hotels, and traveling, but training was basically cost free. The trainers, pros in their respective sports, donated their time to the ICSF for public relations reasons. Pro teams allowed the ICSF to use their facilities in hopes that it would give the athletes who emerged from the camp as champions the incentive to play for the team that helped train them. Private training facilities and gyms all over the country allowed the ICSF use of their sites so they could advertise and promote that they were ICSF partners.

Reid and Buck quickly realized the need to build a facility where they could house and train all ICSF athletes. They would need a site of monstrous proportions with the potential to grow as needed. After searching the country with the help of a real estate developer, they found what they decided was the perfect spot. They chose an old resort in the Catskills situated on hundreds of acres, which in its prime was the ultimate relaxation destination of the "Borsht Belt." A term that described the resort filled area used primarily by vacationing New York Jews in the 1960's. The mountains, although small, were good for skiing, ski jumping, all types of sledding, and mountain climbing. There were lakes for crewing, kayaking, water skiing, and other water sports, along with an existing golf course in need of a serious make-over.

A team of architects was hired to design AllSport. The only instructions they were given were to create two designs: one classic, one contemporary. Both were to include deluxe housing accommodations for one thousand with four cafeterias, two four-star quality restaurants, a state-of-the-art sports medicine and rehab facility, and an administration building with executive offices, boardroom, and an executive dining room. For relaxation purposes, they would build a movie theater and an arcade. The balance of the campus was a mixture of sports domes, arenas, stadiums, fields, and indoor and outdoor aquatic facilities. Horse stables and riding rings, both indoors and out were situated at the edge of the property. There was an area for all racquet sports; tennis, squash, racquetball, and paddle tennis. The golf training facility housed indoor and outdoor driving ranges, chipping and putting areas, bunkers with different types of sand, and a computer-aided driving system. There was even an indoor skiing facility for year-round ski training. Cross-country running/skiing trails weaved their way throughout the campus and the surrounding woods. AllSport was by far the biggest sports training camp in the world, and, as needed, additional buildings, fields, or arenas were designed and constructed. In fact, the original construction crew hired for the ground-breaking was still on the job full time.

Tours were requested so often that a Tour Director, Gina Mattia, was hired with a staff of six. It was common to have as many as four simultaneous tours, and Gina scheduled them as far as six months in advance. Most prospective contributors wanted a tour and they usually wanted it led by Reid. Reid gave tours, but his schedule did not permit many. He tried to give one or two a month. Obviously those were reserved for the heavy hitters, people or companies looking to donate three million or more. These tours were an all-day event. Those on the tour were typically flown in on one of ICSF's helicopters.

After a quick discussion about the facility over breakfast, they started a three-hour morning tour of the campus. Then, following an elaborate lunch in one of AllSport's restaurants, they watched a short film about past champions who AllSport had helped achieve success. After the film the guests got a special treat. They could either watch or participate in whatever sport they chose. This choice was made weeks prior to the tour, so that a competitive game could be scheduled. One team was comprised of teaching pros; the other team included seasoned AllSport athletes. The game, match, or whatever they played, was usually fiercely competitive. Generally, the audience for these games grew to include most of the athletes on campus. It gave up-and-coming champions the chance to strut their stuff. These games were often more competitive and more fun to watch than a pro game, especially when ICSF trainees took the lead. If the touring guest was in shape and wanted to play, he had to sign a waiver beforehand. Depending on the chosen sport, the guest could opt for a one-hour lesson from the top pro on campus at the time. The most requested activity was eighteen holes of golf with Reid.

Finally, the day would end with dinner in the executive dining room. Guests were aware that at this time they were expected to write a check. Then, depending on the size of the donation, they were presented with the coveted ICSF ring. These rings, designed and made by Tiffany's, came in either gold or platinum and had five spots for diamonds. A one million-dollar donor was presented with a gold ring with one diamond in it. When the next million was gifted, a second diamond was inserted. This continued until the ring was full. A five million-dollar contributor received a platinum ring with all five diamonds in place. The rings were worn by most of their owners with pride. They were seen at every society gathering in the country. A simple shake of the hand would let someone know he was in the presence of a member of the elite ICSF club. The club had grown to about 300 members. Once a year they all got together for a fun-filled weekend of activities and dining at AllSport.

3

As Reid had requested, the minute Jay Scott and Buck Green landed, Al escorted them to the executive boardroom. Upon entering the walnut-paneled room, Buck and Jay approached Reid. Jay was close to six foot tall with a slim athletic physique and a receding hairline of short-dark hair. His neatly trimmed goatee gave him an air of intensity. He shook Reid's hand telling him how sorry he was. Buck placed his cigar in an ashtray and gave his friend a bone-crushing bear hug during which both men's eyes filled with tears.

Allowing the emotional moment to pass, Jay said, "I'm going over to the scene now, if any one wants to join me. I'd like to meet back here in an hour. I'm afraid it's going to be a long day, gentlemen."

"I'll come with you, Jay," Al said. "I need to know what's going on, especially if you're going to be using my staff."

After Jay and Al left the room, Buck asked Reid, "Hey, are you sure you're OK?"

"I was until I called Karen. I haven't been able to concentrate since then. I guess I'm kind of numb, but I don't think it's really hit me yet. Buck, I can't believe he's gone. Who the fuck would shoot him and why? I swear, I'm gonna get whoever did this, if it's the last thing I do."

"What you need to do is take it easy. Let Jay handle the investigation. We need to help Art keep this place in control. It's going to get a little messy around here. The press is going to be all over us. It's going to be a media circus, and you, my friend, have to promise me that you won't be too explosive."

"I'll stay calm as long as they don't push me too far."

"No, Reid, it's got to be different this time. The press is going to hound you, but you've got to keep your cool. It's not just your reputation at stake any more. It's AllSport and the entire foundation which have both gotten much bigger than just you and me. We have a lot of people who depend on us to do the right thing. I can help control things when it's just Reid Clark versus the press, but there's too much at stake now."

"You're right."

Buck was silent for a moment. "That's it? No argument? No yelling? No telling me to mind my own business? What are you, getting soft?"

"Yeah, Buck, I guess so," Reid sighed. "This is all just too much for me. You know he was like a brother to me. I feel so damn empty." After a short silence he added, "Buck, I'm going to need you just to be my friend for a few days. Not my agent, just a friend. OK?"

"You got it. Anything you need, I'm here."

Tears welled up in Reid's eyes and trickled down his cheeks. Buck walked over and put a hand on his shoulder.

• • •

While Buck was commiserating with his friend, Jay Scott reached the crime scene, which by this time had been cordoned off with yellow plastic police tape. He flipped his badge at the officer on duty, who responded, "No badge necessary for you, Mr. Scott, go ahead." Jay ducked under the waist-high tape and walked carefully towards the body. The scene was being kept intact until the investigators had inspected everything rigorously.

From behind, Jay heard a loud gruff voice, "Well, if it isn't the infamous Jay Scott; I knew you had to show up sooner or later."

"Hey, Dave," Jay responded to Dave Wheeler, the Chief of Police. "What have we got?"

"Looks like the body was shot elsewhere and dumped here," said Wheeler. "The bullet entered just above the left temple and exited behind the right ear, and took a lot of skull with it. Not a pretty sight. Want to take a look?"

"Yeah, I do. Why do you think he was shot someplace else?"

"Too clean. No blood, no mess. No sign of the displaced skull anywhere. No bullet. Interesting thing is there's no trail of blood either. Like they put a bag or towel over the head, then moved it here and took off the cover."

"Let me see." Jay walked over to the body.

A heavyset man in a light beige suit was crouched next to the body, studying it. He stood and reached to shake Jay's hand, introducing himself in a raspy smoker's voice, "Jim Baxter, County Coroner." Jay shook his hand and introduced himself. "No need, Mr. Scott, we all know who you are."

"Call me Jay. What have you found?"

"Time of death, probably around five a.m. Rigor has started to set in. Body was definitely brought here after death. If I had to guess, we are dealing with a long-range shot from a high-powered rifle. Looks like it entered high and exited low. Probably a sniper shot from a window or rooftop or tree."

"Thanks, Jim. I'll be in touch. I think I'm gonna need a lot of help on this one."

"No problem. I'll be happy to help any way I can."

Chief Wheeler had walked up by this time, and he asked, "Jay, you think it's connected to Reid's threats in any way?"

"It's a strong possibility. I could see the punks from Slam, the gang that threatened Reid, offing someone in retaliation. It would explain why they dumped the body where it would obviously be found. Revenge for locking up one of their members makes sense."

"But why would they kill Bob instead of Reid?"

"Good question, Dave. At this point I'm just thinking out loud."

"Yeah, it looks like you and I are going to be doing a lot of that for a while."

"I'll say. Speaking of that, I hope you're ready to work with me on this one."

"You know me, Jay, I'm a team player."

"Oh right, give me a break. I thought you were going to have a stroke when I brought my guys in to handle security at AllSport after the attempt on Reid."

"I just had to get used to it. This was just a sleepy little town before AllSport. I was used to handling everything on my own. Things have changed and so have I."

"Good, I think we can work together well."

"You'll have the full cooperation of my department. I only hope I can expect the same from your team," said Wheeler.

"What are you implying?"

"Don't play that game with me. You know some of your guys are hotheads. Their elitist attitudes can really piss you off sometimes. My guys complain about them all the time."

"I'll talk to them."

"Good," Wheeler replied.

"In the meantime, we need to figure out where Bob was shot. Have you found any footprints or tread marks?"

"We're working on that now. It'll be tough. There's a lot of traffic around here daily, both foot and vehicle."

"All right, I've seen what I need to for now. Will you join me for a quick meeting with Reid and the others?"

"When?"

"I was hoping *now*, if you can?"

Wheeler thought about it for a moment then said, "All right, I need to ask Reid a few questions anyway." He turned to one of his detectives and said, "Hey, John, come with us."

John Samson was Wheeler's Lieutenant Detective. "Give me a minute," he replied in an annoyed tone.

Jay looked at Wheeler with a raised brow.

Dave quietly answered his implied question. "He's good; he just doesn't like to be interrupted when he's in the middle of an investigation."

Samson was known to be a tough cop. He was about six-two and had a muscular, weightlifter's build. He worked his cases his way and didn't like being told what to do and when. He was smart enough to show his superiors just enough respect to keep them appeased. He had solved enough cases to be given some room and most of the department, including his own men, stayed clear when he was caught up in something.

"Whatever, he's your man," Jay commented.

Samson continued what he was doing for another minute. Jay wasn't sure if he was doing something important or just trying to piss them off. Either way, Jay was getting irritated.

"Al, let's go. Dave, you can come now or join us when he's done, whatever you want."

"We're coming now, just give me a second." Wheeler walked over to Samson and quietly said something.

Samson stood and, a little louder than appropriate, he growled, "Fine!" They both walked over and got in the four-seat golf cart with Jay and Al. John intentionally avoided looking at either of them. Dave decided to hold off on introductions till later.

• • •

When everyone was assembled in the boardroom, Jay looked at Reid. His eyes were red and puffy, obviously from crying. Jay said, "Reid, are you sure you're ready for this?"

"Sure? No. But go ahead, I'll manage."

"OK." Jay turned toward Wheeler. "Dave, this is your show, why don't you brief everyone."

"Thanks, Jay." He looked at the group. "OK, folks, well, the coroner has put the time of death at around five a.m. The last place Bob was seen alive was in a meeting last night in his office. He left late. We're told he usually worked out in one of the campus gyms or went for an early run before coming to the office. I don't think he made it here though. His car is not on the grounds. It looks as if he was shot elsewhere and brought here to be found. I've got two cruisers searching for his car. By the way, Reid, do you have any ideas where we should look besides his condo?"

"He usually stopped for coffee at the deli on Route 78, but I can't imagine he would have done that at five. He usually worked out, then got to the office at around eight-thirty. If he stopped at the deli, it would have been around six."

"Maybe he had an early appointment," Dave replied.

Reid shrugged. "It's possible."

"Have you looked at his calendar?" Buck asked.

"Not yet," said Wheeler.

"OK, Dave, is there anything you need from us?" asked Jay.

"Well, as difficult as this is for me to admit, I'm going to say it. I'd like you to head up this investigation, if you would. We both know this is over my head. I've only dealt with two murders up here, one was the result of a bar fight and the other was domestic; the woman shot her abusive, alcoholic husband in self-defense. This case will be solved much faster if you take the lead. You will have the support of my entire department."

Samson sat quietly, closed his eyes, and slowly shook his head at this statement.

"All right, I'll lead, but I'm going to need total cooperation from *everyone* on your team." He said this looking directly at Samson.

John gave back a blank stare.

Seeing John's cavalier look annoyed Dave. He said, "I told you you'd have it, Jay, and I meant it. If anyone doesn't cooperate, he'll be dealt with."

"Good. OK, Reid, Buck, I'm going to need to use one of the conference rooms as a base office. I'll need some rooms for my people to live in and I'll need one of the choppers. I want to hold a campus-wide meeting ASAP. How quickly can you arrange it, and where?"

"We better do it at Eagle Stadium," Buck said. "It's the only place everyone will fit. I'll get it set up in about an hour. We'll televise it on the campus station in case some people can't make it."

"Very good. Dave, I'd like your team there as well."

"Of course."

"All right." He looked at the clock on the wall. "It's ten after one, and I'd like to hold the meeting at two-thirty, which should last only about a half hour. Then I want to start interviews with Bob's staff. Art, can you spread the word about the meeting?"

"Sure," Art replied.

Everyone left except Reid and Jay. "Reid, if you're up to it, can you call the accounting department and have them ready to meet with us individually around three-fifteen? I'd like to start with the top managers and work down. You said there are about twenty-five people, right?"

"About," Reid said.

"Let's try to schedule each of them for a ten-minute meeting with a ten-minute break after each six interviews. Unless anything extraordinary comes up that will take us till around eight p.m. If you and Buck can handle it, I'd like to have you with me. If not, I'll take care of it."

"No, I need to be part of this. I might get a little emotional every so often, but I've got to do it. For the life of me, I can't understand why this happened. Bob was a good guy."

"Didn't you tell me that Bob was one of your partners in that golf club deal that went bad?" Jay asked.

"Yeah, so?"

"Didn't you list the other partners as possible suspects when *you* started receiving threats?"

"Yes, but that was *my* deal. The others were upset with me for not keeping the deal alive with more funding. Bob was only a small investor, and they had no problem with *him*."

"But it is a possibility, right?"

"I guess anything is possible, but I just don't see it," said Reid.

"I'm only trying to prove a point. There is probably no connection, but we have to look at every possibility."

"You have nothing to prove to me. You're here because I'm convinced you're the right guy for the job. Do what you need to do."

"That's the right attitude, but you're not going to like what I have to do. When you're ready, and the sooner the better, I need to interview you. You and Bob were close for a long time. I'm sure you'll reveal things that will help the investigation without even realizing it. Just let me know when you're ready. OK?"

"Sure. Maybe we can do it tonight. Let's see how the other interviews go."

"Right." Jay looked at his watch. "We should get over to the stadium since it's almost time."

"Let me call Lisa in accounting and then we can go."

Reid dialed the phone and informed Lisa of the interview schedule. He also inquired if she knew about the meeting at Eagle Stadium. Of course she knew. If there was one thing about Art, he got the job done quickly.

Reid and Jay left the boardroom and headed to the stadium. As they were driving in the cart, Jay said, “Do me a favor, just like you did when you were threatened. Start making a mental list of anyone you know that had any issues with Bob or you. Here use this.” He handed Reid a pen.

“I can’t write them now. I’ll make the list later.”

“It’s not a pen, it’s a recorder. Just push the button and speak near the top. It should help as things pop into your head as I’m sure they will.”

Reid pushed the button, held the pen to his mouth and quietly said, “This really sucks!”

He pushed the button on the other end and they listened to his recorded voice.

“I agree,” Jay sighed.

They pulled up to the stadium entrance and made their way to the door through the entering crowd.

4

About eighty percent of the campus was already seated and the remainder was filing in quickly. Reid and Jay joined Buck, Al, Art, Dave, and his men near the podium on the field. Jay looked up to see a huge video screen behind them showing whoever was at the podium.

Buck spoke into the microphone. "Folks, we're going to start as soon as everyone is here; it should be about five more minutes."

The crowd had hushed as he spoke and slowly their conversations resumed. Jay said to the group around him, "I'm going to be giving some instructions about how to handle the press as well as some other things. I think one of you should open it up, though."

"I'm going to open," Reid said without hesitation.

The others were quiet. Buck asked, "Are you sure you're up to it?"

Reid just nodded his head and walked to the podium. "May I have your attention, please?"

Respectful silence immediately engulfed the stadium. "Thank you. By now I'm sure most of you have heard, Bob Thomas, our Chief Financial Officer and my dear friend, was murdered this morning." Gasps were heard in different pockets of the crowd. "I know many of you were fond of Bob. He probably worked out with many of you at one time or another. I know it was one of the things he enjoyed most about AllSport. I will tell you that Bob often spoke about the time he spent with many of you. Your drive and determination always uplifted him. I'm sorry to drop this on you all in such an impersonal way, but there was really no other way to do it. Bob was a good man and I'm having some trouble understanding how and why this happened, but it has and now we have to deal with it. I'm going to bring Private Investigator, Jay Scott, up to the podium now. He, along with our local Police Chief, Dave Wheeler, will be running the investigation. I expect full cooperation from each and every one of you. Before Jay starts, I'd like everyone to bow their heads for a moment of silence in memorial to Bob." Reid put his head down and everyone followed. Quiet sobs could be heard throughout the audience.

Jay let some time pass and then walked over, put is hand on Reid's shoulder, and relieved him from the podium.

"Ladies and gentlemen, I'm very sorry for your grief. I don't like to give instructions in this manner, but I don't have any choice. First and foremost, the press is going to be all over this. I know some of you would like to be on the news but, please, out of respect to Bob and ICSF as a whole, please do not give any interviews.

"I will be holding press conferences daily and informing them of where we stand in the investigation. I would prefer if anyone approaches you, that you refer them to me, Reid, or Buck. I will also be setting up a team to interview each of you, one at a time. Please cooperate and be punctual. It will help us tremendously. If any of you have any information about the situation, please come forward immediately. If you have seen or heard anything suspicious or out of the ordinary, I'd like to know about it right away. By later today I will have an anonymous tip program in place. We will also be offering a financial reward for anyone with information that leads to an arrest.

"I would appreciate if everyone on campus at this time would plan to stay on campus for the next week, at least. If you have previous plans to leave already in place, please see me after this meeting so we can schedule your interview before you leave. This includes any of you pro's. I'm sorry for the inconvenience but we have no choice. My door will be open to all of you twenty-four hours a day. If you prefer to be discreet, feel free to call me on my cell. My business cards with my cell number will be handed out at the door on your way out. Before I dismiss you, let me quickly introduce Dave Wheeler, The Chief of Police." He motioned for Dave to join him.

Dave walked to the podium and Jay whispered to him, "Go ahead, say a few words, it'll be good for your team to hear that we are sharing the lead on this."

Dave nodded then stepped up to the microphone. "Good afternoon, I'm Chief Wheeler. I know this is a difficult time for you all, so I'll be quick. I want to thank you for your quiet attention at this briefing. As you heard, we will be around for a while, and in fact, we will be all over the campus. AllSport has done great things for this community and we would like to wrap this case up as fast as we can. To do so we will need your help. Please cooperate with anyone working on the case. It may at times interfere with your daily routine, but with your cooperation it will all be over quickly and we'll be out of your way. Until then, expect to see security guards, police officers, and investigators everywhere on campus and around town. *We're* on *your* side, please make sure *you're* on *our* side. Thank you."

Buck walked up and took Dave's place. "For any of you who don't know me, I'm Buck Green. If you're lucky, one day I'll represent you, *then* you'll know fame and fortune. I say this not as a joke, for this is certainly no time for joking. I say it to remind you of one thing: each and every one of you is extremely privileged.

Your talent in your sport has resulted in your invitation by the ICSF to train here at AllSport. You need to remember that this is a privilege and you should be thankful for it. There is nothing any of us want more than for every one of you to achieve success. At that time, you can be as big a media magnet or star as you wish. If you don't yet understand what I'm implying, let me be more direct. The media is going to be all over this as Mr. Scott has said. Some of you may see it as an opportunity to jump-start your career. Although a little on-air time might seem attractive, it is not. No one is to give any interviews or allow any filming without our involvement. If anyone thinks I'm not serious about this, you are mistaken. If any of you are found to have talked to the media in any fashion during this investigation, you will be finished at AllSport. Please don't make that mistake. Bob had a big role in helping AllSport become what it is today. In fact, without his help, most of you probably wouldn't be here. Remember that as you remember him. As a last note, the camp psychologist, Dr. Haber, will be available around the clock if any of you just need to talk. We will be in touch with each of you. In the meantime, try to go about your regular training schedule. It will help us if everything remains as normal as possible on campus. Thank you for your time."

When the crowd started to leave the stadium, Jay said to Buck, "Will you come with us? I have to interview the accounting department and I'd like you and Reid with me."

"Sure I can do it, but let's leave Reid alone for a while. He needs some time."

"I already recommended that to him. He insists on being involved," Jay responded.

Reid approached and said, "We better go; we've got a tight schedule and the interviews start in five minutes. That's just enough time to get back to the boardroom. Have you guys eaten anything? I'm pretty hungry since I haven't really felt like eating all day, but I'm starting to get a headache."

"I only had a light breakfast, so I'm kind of hungry," said Jay.

"Yeah, me too," Buck replied.

"What do you want? I'll get Nancy to order from The Winners Circle," said Reid.

"How about a grilled chicken Caesar salad," Buck suggested.

"Sounds good, I'll have the same," Jay agreed.

Reid radioed Nancy to place the order. "Hey, Nanc, are you doing OK?"

"A little better, I guess. It comes and goes," she replied.

"Yeah, I know, I'd let you go home but we're going to need you to handle calls from the press when they start coming in."

"We've had one already. The Channel Two reporter called looking for either of you. They're on the way. I asked how he knew about this already. He said he got an anonymous tip."

"*Great.* So much for peace and quiet. Hey, do me a favor, and call Johnny and order a chef salad and two chicken Caesars. We'll pick them up on our way back. We're going to be using the boardroom for interviews all afternoon. If Lisa gets there before us, tell her we'll be right up."

"She's here already."

"Oh, OK, we'll see you in a few minutes."

Reid said to Buck and Jay, "Well, word's out. Channel Two is on the way now. We better give Al instructions on how his team should handle the press."

"Tell him to meet us in the office immediately," Jay replied.

Buck radioed Al, who said he was finishing up with Chief Wheeler and would be up as quickly as possible.

"Tell him to ask Dave to come up too," Jay added.

After Buck gave Al the instructions, Jay said, "I need to handle Dave with kid gloves. I want his help, but as you saw with Samson, some of his guys are going to be pissed that I'm running the case. I can't afford any dissension. So if it seems like I'm pussy-footing around with them, it's because *I am*."

Reid stopped the cart in front of The Winners Circle, one of the campus restaurants. It was a favorite hangout for the athletes with colorful, futuristic décor and huge-screen TVs everywhere. A push of a button from either side of the dining tables raised a flat screen TV through a slot. Although satellite brought in live sports from all around the world, most athletes came to play QB1, or one of NTN's many other interactive television games. Things became very active in the restaurant when people were playing QB1 during a televised professional or college football game.

Autographed sports memorabilia covered the walls and ceiling. Jerseys, balls, racquets, helmets, skates, pucks, bats; it was all there. It was said that, if the equipment were sold at auction, it would probably raise about five million dollars. Every dish on the menu was named after an athlete who left AllSport to become a pro or Olympian.

Reid picked up the salads and drove back to the office.

5

Lisa Difillipi, was one of Bob's protégés. Along with being a financial wizard, she, unlike most accountants, had a very special way with people. She could speak with ICSF benefactors about making good on their pledges without offending them. She was an intense worker when in the office and a party animal when not.

She was just hanging up the phone as Reid, Buck, and Jay entered the boardroom. She said, "That was Barry, my Accounts Payable manager. He just received a call from a News Seven reporter. Don't worry, he didn't answer any questions, he just referred the reporter up here."

"We've got about half an hour till the news vans are lined up at the front gate," Jay said. "We need Art and Dave here as soon as possible."

Reid hit the intercom. "Nancy, please tell Art and Dave to come up."

"All right," she replied.

Jay walked over to Lisa and introduced himself.

"I know who you are, Mr. Scott. I think everyone on campus does. This place has changed a lot since you took over security."

"I hope you agree that it's safer than before?"

"Well, before Reid's threats, we never really worried about safety. AllSport had a very relaxed atmosphere. The worst thing that happened was an occasional fight between some athletes. With your guys around, there is little chance of that any more. Some of your guys get a little overzealous once in a while, and in fact, sometimes they scare the hell out of me."

"Oh, really?" Jay said with genuine concern. "Please tell me who is bothering you and how. They will be immediately dealt with."

"I'd rather not go into it right now. I'd really rather just answer your questions and get back to my office. The whole department is understandably on edge and emotional right now. And, quite frankly, everyone is a little nervous about coming up here. I need to be there to keep things from falling apart."

"Hey, where is Joe Spinelli?" Jay asked, looking at a list. "This list shows he's not here. Isn't he second in command of the department?"

"He's on vacation in Nepal. Reid put me in charge this morning, until he's back. I tried to call Joe on his cell, but I just got his voicemail. Reid asked me to tell him to come back immediately, but I didn't say that in the message. I just said it was important that he calls me as soon as possible. I doubt he'll have any reception where he is. I think it's a pretty sure bet that there aren't many cell towers in Nepal."

"Nepal? What's he doing there? Climbing Everest?" Jay asked with a grin.

"You got it," Lisa said.

"Really? I was kidding. Climbing expeditions up Everest are pretty expensive." Jay looked at Buck. "Spinelli's got a big salary?"

"No, not really."

"He's always saving for his next vacation," Lisa said. "He loves adventures. His last vacation was extreme skiing, before that was whitewater rafting, bungee jumping, and sky-diving. Makes the rest of our vacations seem kind of boring, huh?"

"I'd prefer to call it relaxing," Buck said.

"I think *we'll* try to get in touch with Joe," Jay said. "It might be better coming from us. Besides, you are going to have your hands full with the rest of the department. I want to ask some quick questions before I let you go back, OK?"

"Sure, that's why I'm here, right?" Lisa said with a shrug.

"First, I would like you to start making a list of anything out of the ordinary you may have seen or heard lately in accounting. Include any arguments or disagreements Bob may have had with anyone. Think hard about any strange phone calls that were made or anyone you don't know that was in the office. If you can bring me back a list by the end of the day, I'd appreciate it."

"OK, but there are a couple of things I can tell you right now."

"Please do."

"Well, Bob was always arguing with Karen, his wife, and they fought all the time. I'm sure you know about their problems already."

"No, I don't. Why don't you fill me in?"

"I figured Reid had already explained it, but if you want me to, I will."

They all looked at Reid who said, "Just haven't gotten to it yet. Go ahead, Lisa, tell them."

"Well, about a year ago, Karen caught Bob having an affair. In fact, Bob's girlfriend was living with him up here during the week. It was pretty messy. Bob ended the affair, but the only way Karen would take him back was if he put both houses and all their assets in her name. I guess he really loved her because he actually did it."

She looked over at Reid who was slowly nodding. "It gets worse," he said. "She also made him take out a five-million dollar life insurance policy. She was understandably pissed off. To top it off, his ex-girlfriend made what I *would* have called idle threats when he dumped her. She really thought he was going to leave his wife and marry her. She basically stalked him for a couple of months. It was strange."

"So it looks like we have at least two prime suspects at the moment. I'll get Joel to follow up with Karen. I'll make sure he's discreet in case she's innocent. It's difficult to investigate a spouse, because even when they're guilty they always play up the fragile, grief-stricken role. It's usually hard to tell whether the tears are real or forced. Joel is the best investigator I've seen at reading people's emotions. As far as the ex-girlfriend is concerned, does anyone know her whereabouts?"

"No idea. I know she moved out of the area but I have no clue where," Reid said. "I think her family lives in New Jersey and has a summer house up here."

"What's her name?" Jay asked.

"Diane something," Reid said, tapping the table with his fingers. "What the hell was her last name? Diane...Diane...Diane Powers, that's it, Diane Powers."

"Good," Jay said. "I'll get Dave to follow up locally and Stu will check out the family in New Jersey."

Jay turned towards Lisa. "Lisa, thank you for your time; you've been very helpful. Please remember to work on the list for me. I'm sure things will pop into your mind as you go about your daily routine. I often get the best information after my interviews are over. By the way, is anyone else out today besides Joe?"

"Yeah, a couple of our auditors are out. We always give them a break after an intense audit. They'll be back the day after tomorrow."

"All right, we're good for now. You can head back. Thanks again, Lisa."

"Glad to help," Lisa said as she got up.

Buck nodded at Lisa, saying, "We'll keep you informed. Thanks again."

As she left, Reid pushed the intercom, "Nancy, will you call Art again and get him up here, please."

"He's right next to me, Reid. He and Chief Wheeler have been waiting; they're on their way in."

"OK, thank you."

Before Fornham and Wheeler even sat down, Jay began, "Gentlemen, I'm sure you're aware that a media blitz is imminent. There is one news van already at the gate and…."

"Make that three," Art interrupted. "Two more showed up while you were meeting with Lisa."

"Shit…OK, I want a security escort with every news team that comes on site. Art, tell your guys to stay with them wherever they go. No one is to interfere with the crime scene. If they want to film it, they do it from behind the barrier. No athletes or trainers are to be interviewed. They can film as much of the camp as they want. When they want an interview, they can come see me. Absolutely no one else on campus is to speak with them. OK?"

"You got it," Art said on his way out.

"Dave, can you come with me to my office. Reid doesn't need to hear the details," Jay asked.

"What?" Reid's irritation flared. "Enough with being delicate for my sake. I appreciate the concern for my feelings, but cut it out. I want to be involved with every aspect of this investigation. I may get upset at times, but I owe it to Bob to help find the son of a bitch who did this."

"All right Reid, if you say so," Jay responded. He turned to look at Wheeler. "What have you heard from the coroner?"

"He confirmed that, due to the size and angle of entry and exit wounds, along with the quantity of dislodged brain mass, the bullet came from a sniper's rifle from about 80 feet away and at least 20 feet above the ground. We're combing the area around the deli for evidence of the kill site or sniper's position. We're canvassing rooftops and all empty office spaces for shells or residue. His personal effects including his wallet have all been searched and recorded. Nothing found worth discussing."

"OK, before we take the next interview, I want to review what we've got so far. I just found out that we need to locate and question Bob's ex-girlfriend."

"I thought he was married," Dave said.

"He was. Both his wife and his ex-mistress just became prime suspects. His wife caught him having an affair last year and took him back only after setting some pretty strict stipulations. She took control of all their assets and, if he strayed again, she would keep it all. She also made him increase his life insurance policy."

Dave's eyebrows rose.

"Interesting, huh? Well, it gets even better; it turns out the girlfriend went a little nuts after he dumped her; she actually started stalking him. Dave, we need to find her right away. I'll send a team to New Jersey. You put a team on her trail up here. Her name is Diane Powers."

"Good, it'll give Samson something to do besides give me a hard time."

"Why is he giving *you* trouble?" Jay asked.

Dave shrugged. "He thinks I'm kissin' your ass."

Jay frowned as he muttered, "Oh. Well, sometimes being a smart cop looks like ass-kissing to an immature cop. John may be a good detective but he's also obviously very immature."

"Look, all I care about is solving this case. If having you in the lead speeds things up, then it's the right thing to do. I don't really give a damn what anyone thinks about it. It was my decision to make and I made it. A quick close on this will look good on my resume anyway."

"That is the right attitude and you made the right decision.

In fact, after this is over, *if* things go well, you may have some options open up to you. I've been known to hire detectives onto my team after working cases with them. Some of them are pretty wealthy now."

Dave looked at Jay and raised his brow and nodded.

Jay just said, "We'll see."

"I better get going before we have a complete media circus here," Dave said. "I'll let you know if we find the Powers girl." He turned and left.

Buck, who'd been silently observing the discussions, hit the intercom, "Who's next, Nancy?"

"Cynthia Lopez is on her way in now, Buck."

Cynthia came in and went through the same Q & A session Lisa had. The next two interviews revealed nothing new.

The men ate their salads during the next few interviews. They spoke with each other about some of the interviews during their breaks. The next ten interviews were relatively quick and uninformative. With only four to go, the three men needed a bathroom break. As they walked by Nancy on the way back into the boardroom, they heard the elevator doors open. They turned to see Linda Caruso and a cameraman get off the elevator and head quickly in their direction.

Linda was one of the few respectable reporters on the air. She was a good-looking woman with bold features, perfect for TV. She commanded the screen and exuded power as she controlled her interviews. All three men had been interviewed by Linda at one time or another. Jay was a little irritated. He yelled, "Linda! How the hell did you get up here?" Without giving her a chance to answer he said, "You know what, forget it. Don't even answer that question. It's a good thing I like your tenacity. I would throw any other reporter outta here. Quite honestly, I don't know if one of our guards could handle you anyway. I'll make you a deal; if you promise to ask very simple questions, I'll give you an interview right now."

"You got it, Jay. Tell me as soon as you're ready. Can I get all three of you in the shot?"

"Not me," Reid said. "I'm not ready for this yet."

"And you, Buck?" Linda asked.

"Never backed away from a camera before. Why start now?"

"OK, Tom, tell me when you're ready to shoot…Oooh!" She made a face as she caught her poor use of wording.

"Excuse me, gentlemen, I wasn't thinking."

"No problem, let's just do it," Jay said.

"OK, everybody ready?"

Buck and Jay nodded. Tom said, "Ready."

Linda cleared her throat, held up her microphone, and looked at the camera. "Roll it."

The camera's light went on and Linda began, "I'm here in the executive offices of AllSport with Buck Green, Co-Founder and Co-Chairman of The Inner City Sports Foundation, and Jay Scott, Private Investigator and Security Consultant to AllSport. Good afternoon, gentlemen. First, please accept my condolences on the death of Bob Thomas, your Chief Financial Officer. Jay, I heard Bob was murdered. Do you have any suspects yet?"

"Well, Linda, let me congratulate you on your remarkable ability to get the first interview. I will be holding a press conference tomorrow morning, at which time I will explain some of our developments. For now, let's just say that our investigation is in its early stages. We are currently following a few possible leads and scouring the crime scene. I feel fairly confident that we will bring this case to a rapid close, at which time Bob's killer will be brought to justice."

"You say you have a few leads. What are the names of the suspects?"

"*Linda*," Jay said in a warning tone.

"All right, all right," she said, backing off.

She turned to Buck. "Mr. Green, as Co-Chairman of ICSF and AllSport, can you tell me how this tragedy will affect things here at the camp?"

"Sure, Linda. We had a campus-wide meeting this morning and we discussed that all training activities will continue right through the investigation. ICSF has become the nation's foremost charitable foundation and we have a responsibility to our contributors, our athletes, and the entire country to maintain continuity of our daily program here. All staff members have helped set goals for themselves and their area of work, and they all have competitive backgrounds in some sport. We have all worked hard to create a culture of teamwork, and sincerely believe that our efforts at AllSport make a big difference in three major areas. We help underprivileged, talented kids achieve levels of success they never would have had a chance at without us. Our efforts have raised the level of competition in all professional American sports. And finally we have helped America win more Gold Medals in both the winter and summer Olympics than ever before. I have no doubt in my mind that Bob Thomas would want us to continue our efforts without any interruptions. I hope that answers your question sufficiently."

"Quite," said Linda. "Thank you both for your time. I'm Linda Caruso reporting on the tragic death of Bob Thomas, AllSport's CFO, here in the Catskills."

Tom turned off the camera and Linda reached to shake all three men's hands. "Gentlemen, thank you again. I'll be going now. I don't want to overstay my welcome."

As they were heading back to the elevator, Jay said, "Oh, by the way, Linda, you will be met by one of our security guards as you get off the elevator. You are welcome to film the campus as long as you are with a guard. If you decide to escape *this* guard's companionship as you did the last guard assigned to you, you will be escorted off campus and will never be allowed on again. Do I make myself clear?"

"Crystal, Jay." She waved and entered the elevator.

"Let's go finish up," Jay said walking towards the boardroom. "You guys go in, and I'll be there in two minutes. I want to call Joel and Stu and get them working on our lady friends."

As Reid and Buck passed Nancy on the way to the boardroom, she said, "Reid, are you OK? You look a little pale."

"I'll be all right. Thanks Nancy."

"Joanne Minkoff is in there waiting for you. After her interview, you only have two left."

"Good," Buck said. "I can't take much more of this. Can we go get a steak or something afterwards? That salad was good but it didn't put a dent in my appetite."

"Whatever you want, Buck," Reid said with his head hung low.

"Hey, are you gonna hold up? Why don't you sit the last few out? Go lie down in your office. Jay and I will finish up and then we'll get out of here."

"I think I will, thanks." As he walked back past Nancy, he said, "I'm gonna go lie down for a while."

"What can I get you?" she asked quietly.

"Nothing, thanks. I just need some rest."

He went into his office, shut the door, turned off the lights, and lay down on the couch. When he closed his eyes the emotions of the day swept over him and he began to cry.

After a few moments, he just lay there thinking. Who the hell could have done this? The more he thought about it, the more twisted his thoughts became. Suddenly he sat up and said, "Oh, my God, that's it." He couldn't believe he hadn't thought of it earlier. He had to tell Jay immediately. When he entered the boardroom, he was about to blurt out his thoughts when he saw that they were in the middle of another interview. He shook hands with Pat Jackson, another manager in accounting.

"Sorry for interrupting," Reid apologized.

"It's all right," Jay said. "Please continue, Pat."

"Well, it was at least ten months ago. There was a huge fight in the gym while Bob was working out. He said it looked like the two athletes were going to kill each other. He said if he weren't there to stop it, one of them probably would have died. Hector Vasquez, a Columbian-born boxer from Miami, was stabbed by Bill Faxton, a basketball player from L.A. Bob actually threatened to hit Faxton with a steel bar from the weight-lifting area. A few months before the fight, Faxton had been caught stealing equipment from AllSport and selling it on Ebay. Bob made sure he was not only thrown out of camp but also arrested for both the stabbing and the theft. Vasquez was given a warning that next time he would be thrown out also. Both Faxton and Vasquez were in street gangs before coming to AllSport. I've heard that most gangs believe once a brother, always a brother. I know Bob received a call from one of Faxton's fellow gang members. The gang is comprised totally of street basketball players, who call themselves, 'The Judges,' a catchy way of saying they rule the court. Faxton is still in jail, but maybe another gang member killed Bob."

"Pat, did Bob tell you what was said during that phone call?" Jay asked. "Was he threatened?"

"I'm not sure. He didn't want to talk about it. All he said was that he got the call."

"I know what was said," Reid interjected. "Why don't you let Pat go? I've got some other stuff to tell you and I'll go over the call too."

"OK, Pat, thanks for your help. Call us if you think of anything else," Jay said.

Pat walked out and Jay shut the door.

"Well?" Jay said looking at Reid.

"The phone call came just after the fight. It was quick. The guy said that Faxton better not end up in jail or else. Then he hung up...I guess our suspect list is building quickly. Isn't it?"

"Yeah, but I remember a similar list that grew even faster a few years ago," Jay said, referring to the list of possible suspects during Reid's death threat investigation. "You still wear the crown for the longest list of people with reason to do you bodily harm."

"Obviously not something I'm proud of. But forget that, I've got another possible suspect for Bob's list. I just remembered another old situation that may be relevant. About six years ago Bob was consulting for a company down on Wall Street. He found a big discrepancy in the balance sheet, and after further investigation he proved that the missing funds had been stolen by one of the partners. Bob blew the whistle and the guy got a five-year sentence. We heard that his wife divorced him right away and got everything. The timing is perfect. Busted six years ago, five-year sentence, divorced, no house, no money. He's fresh out of prison and probably pissed off. It adds up, right?"

"I'll say! What's his name? I'll get someone on him immediately."

"I've been trying to remember. It was something very proper, you know, one of those sophisticated names that get you beat up as kid. Think of some. If you say it, I'll know it."

Buck chimed in, "How about Alfred, Charles, or Frederick."

Jay threw out a few, "Jefferson, Burton, Nelson, Edward...."

"Edward, it's something like that. What the hell was it? Edward, Edmund, Edwin, that's it," Reid shouted, "Edwin Riley."

"Any idea where they put him away?" Jay asked.

"No, where do they put people from Wall Street for white collar crime. Probably some country-club type prison?"

"There are a few possibilities, but I'll find out. Do you remember his company or where he lived?"

"The company was some small boutique investment house. He lived in Purchase. The house was enormous. Probably worth at least five million. Bob drove me by it one day after we played golf at Westchester Country Club. It was only a few minutes away from the club."

"OK, let's finish up our last interview," Buck said.

Buck pushed the intercom. "Nancy, is the next one here?"

"Yes, should I send him in?"

"Please."

"OK, his name is Isaac," Nancy informed them.

"Nancy, it's been a long tough day. Why don't you go home and get some rest. Come in at nine tomorrow instead of eight."

Isaac came in, sat down, and immediately started talking. He was like a talking accounting textbook, full of trivia and boring facts. He spoke of how Bob was his mentor. "He helped me with everything from accounting to women. I'm really going to miss him. He made working in accounting fun, if you can believe that." After ten minutes the three men had heard enough. Isaac was a nice guy, but they couldn't get him to shut up.

Finally, Jay couldn't take it any more and interrupted him. "OK, Isaac, thank you, you've been a big help. Good night."

"You mean I'm done?"

"Yes, go home, have a good night," Jay said.

"Is there anything else I can do to help?"

"Not right now but thanks," Jay said. "We'll be in touch if we need you."

"OK then, I guess I'll go." Disappointed, Isaac shook all their hands and left.

"Whew! Good job, Jay. I thought he'd never stop," Buck said.

"Now let's get out of here and get a steak someplace where there's no reporters, no accountants, and no athletes."

"Hey!" Reid yelped.

"Sorry about that, but you play *golf*," Buck kidded.

"What's that supposed to mean?"

"Forget it; it was a bad attempt at humor. I think we're all a little slap-happy by now."

"Speak for yourself," Jay retaliated in jest.

"All right, all right, truce. Enough already, let's go," Buck said. "I'll drive one of the Hummers."

6

Though the food at AllSport's restaurants was better than any other in the area, they really wanted to get off campus. Reid and Jay were on their cell phones for most of the twenty-minute ride.

They slid onto the black leather benches of a private booth in the back of the Deer Park Tavern and ordered a porterhouse big enough for the three of them to share. Buck perused the wine list and ordered a bottle of Pinot Noir. They all needed to loosen up a little. As they drank the first glass, they discussed the day. Jay explained that his team was following up all the leads that had surfaced.

He then looked at Reid and said, "Hey, I know Bob was your good friend, and it's obvious you're pretty badly shaken. But I need you to snap out of it as quickly as you can. I hate to put it this way, but you can mourn later. I need leads right now and there stuck someplace in your head. We can't afford to wait until I hear these things from other people. You knew about each of the situations discussed today, but you're letting emotions cloud your mind. If you want to catch Bob's killer, and I know you do, you need to think hard. Write down anything that comes to mind, no matter how trivial it seems."

Reid stared at Jay in disbelief before verbally lashing out. "How dare you, Jay. I have been with you all fucking day. I have been holding back all my emotions so that I can help. Do you know how badly I'm hurting right now? Of course I'm not thinking clearly. My best friend was shot today at *my* camp, and his body was found during a tour that I was giving to the President of the United States. You think I'm letting my emotions cloud my mind. Damn right I am. In fact, I'm surprised my mind is working at all. It's taken every bit of strength I've got just to hold back the tears. If you want my help, you'd better change your attitude towards me. Give me a break."

Neither Jay nor Buck said a word during Reid's tirade. When he finished, Jay put up his hands in surrender. "I apologize, Reid. I was wrong. I don't know what I was thinking. Please forgive me."

Reid closed his eyes for a moment before letting out a sigh. "This has been a difficult day for you too. I will do the best that I can, but I can't just turn off my emotions. I'm not built like that."

"I know. Take your time. Give me whatever you can whenever you can."

Buck filled everyone's glass and said, "Well, gentlemen, it seems we're all a little tense. Drink up; we obviously all need it." The steak arrived and Buck ordered another bottle of wine.

After finishing dinner, Reid said, "You know what I'd like to do? Go back, get some cigars, and take a walk around camp. Usually at this time of night, you get to see a lot of deer and other wildlife that roam the woods up here. What do you think?"

"I'm game," said Jay.

"Good one, Jay," Buck said, laughing. "I'm in too."

"What's so funny?"

"Reid was talking about wildlife and you said I'm game. Tell me you didn't mean it."

"I'd love to take credit for being witty, but it really wasn't intentional."

"C'mon, let's go," Reid said, getting up. They went out and gave the valet the ticket for their vehicle.

"There's been a news van parked behind your H2 for about half an hour," the valet said. "I'm afraid you're not going to be able to avoid them. Too bad the Hummer has AllSport written on the side."

"Thanks for the warning," Reid said. "Hey, what kind of car does Roy drive?"

"Who?" asked the valet.

"The owner of the restaurant."

"Oh, right. A Jaguar and it's over there. Why?"

"Don't get our truck yet, I'll be right back." Reid ran back into the restaurant and found the owner. They had a quick discussion and shook hands. Reid ran back out to the valet. "Roy is going to take the Hummer home tonight and we're going to use his car. Will you get it for us, please?"

"Sure, let me just verify it with him first."

The valet headed inside.

Buck chuckled. "Good thinking. I'd like to see the look on the reporter's face when Roy gets in the Hummer later."

The valet came out and brought them the Jaguar.

When they got back to AllSport, they stopped at Buck's office and grabbed a few Monte Cristos, direct from Havana, of course. He kept two humidors filled with them. It was rare to see Buck without a cigar.

The sharp blue flame of Buck's windproof torch lit their cigars effortlessly in spite of the breeze. It was a crisp, clear evening. Reid led the walk, following a paved path through the center of campus. They passed between campus housing buildings and continued to the aquatic center, which was a magnificent sight at night. One full side of the three-story building was glass. Comfortable benches just off the path provided a spectacular view. There were usually people sitting and watching divers practice on the three-meter platform. Lanterns washed the building in soft blue light without creating a glare, classical music quietly played in the background. The calming effect drew many athletes after a grueling day of training.

The men sat and watched without a word. It just so happened that Marco DeCappa was training tonight, and he was expected to bring home multiple gold medals in the upcoming Olympics. He was the most graceful diver the sport had ever seen. They watched his first dive, a reverse two-and-a-half with a full twist. Reid and Buck smiled as Jay almost jumped out of his seat in excitement.

"Did you see that? My God, it was incredible!" He settled back onto the bench only to jump back up after the next dive. "Wow, I've never seen anything like this. I mean, I've watched it on TV, but I never really paid any attention. It's absolutely unbelievable."

"You're watching the best diver in the world. It's hard to appreciate some sports on TV. Watching live is entirely different; much more exciting. Marco does a few dives that no one else has ever performed. He just started his session. His dives will get more difficult as he warms up. Let's watch for a while, then head over to the martial arts arena. Our recruiters have scheduled a Tae-Kwondo demonstration tonight between our trainers, who are some of the best in the country."

"To tell you the truth, I think I'd rather stay here and watch Marco. I've seen enough Tae-Kwondo fights to last a lifetime. In fact, I'm pretty sure that, if you put my guys in the ring with yours, the sure bet would be with mine."

"Reid, Jay is a black belt himself. In *how many* styles of fighting?" Buck asked, looking at Jay.

"Three, but I haven't fought in years. I didn't fight for sport, only for survival. Anyway, if you don't mind, I think watching

Marco will be much more relaxing."

"No problem," Reid answered.

They sat back and watched Marco perform his next dive. As Reid had predicted, the dive was more complicated than the previous dives. "Unbelievable!" exclaimed Jay.

They all finished their cigars and Buck reached into his jacket pocket for three more. After lighting them, Reid said, "Can we walk a little? If I sit here any longer I'm going to doze off." They agreed and stood to walk. "Golf course or lake? Any preference, Jay?"

"Let's walk around the lake. I'd rather walk the course during the day when we can play it." He looked at his watch. "It's ten-forty, so let's walk for about an hour and then I've got to get some sleep. I have to head out early. Do we need to call the pilot tonight for a chopper around seven-thirty?"

"Yes, I'll have Al call him." Buck radioed Al and gave him the information.

"Where are you headed, Jay?" Reid asked as they started walking.

"Well, originally I was going to have Joel and Stu follow up on Bob's wife and girlfriend, but I've changed my mind. I'm gonna put them on Faxton. If he's the killer, it could get dangerous. I know they can handle it so I'm putting Jody Macintire on Karen. She knows how to handle a situation like this with a spouse. Jody can subtly get a confession out of a guilty party without offending them if they are innocent. Even I don't know how she does it. Dave will follow up on Diane Powers up here, and I've got a team working on finding her in New Jersey. I'm going to Wall Street, and then up to Westchester to follow up on our friend Edwin.

"I'm bringing a team of four up here to start interviewing everyone else on campus. I want to make sure that no one leaves before we get a chance to speak with everyone: athletes, trainers, and the entire staff. We need to know immediately if anyone decides to leave without our permission. I hate to do it, but just like last time, I'm going to put a team around the perimeter of the camp. I have already talked to Al; he's checking every vehicle that leaves, including news vans and delivery trucks. Hopefully we can wrap this up quickly, so people don't get too upset."

"Hopefully," Reid agreed. "Last time it didn't go very smoothly. Some of our more unruly athletes began to feel a little cooped up. When they get restless, they can get mean. The last thing we need is fighting to start on campus while the news coverage is at its height."

"The best way to avoid that is to close the case quickly. I'll do my best, gentlemen."

"We know you will," Buck said. "What do you need from us while you're away?"

"Reid, I know I was insensitive earlier and I'm sorry. But I really need you both to think hard about any other situations, recent or in the past, which may be relevant in any way. You've been through this before and you both know knowledge is power in any investigation. The more information I have, the better and faster I can do my job. Try to have a written list for me when I get back tomorrow evening."

They had walked about halfway around the lake, and it was extremely dark and quiet. The trees on the trail at this point formed a tunnel known on campus as spook hollow. It was more than a little creepy. Buck and Reid had walked it fairly often, but it was Jay's first experience. Reid noticed that Jay had not only quieted down but had quickened his pace. Suddenly the silence was broken by something in the trees. There was movement everywhere and large things flying and swooping in all directions. Jay let out a yelp and started running. Reid and Buck fell apart laughing and followed him out of the tunnel. They finally caught up to him and they all had to sit down and catch their breath.

"What the hell was that?" Jay asked, gasping for air.

"Turkeys," they both answered simultaneously, still laughing.

"*Turkeys*! I thought we were under attack. Son of a bitch! Turkeys! I can't believe it. OK, you've both had your kicks at my expense. Promise me this doesn't go beyond us. If my people get wind of this, I'll never hear the end of it. I'll be shamed for life. *Turkeys!*"

Reid chuckled. "You're safe with me."

Buck was silent.

Jay raised his brow. "Buck?"

"I don't know, Jay. You know I always like to have a little dirt on everyone. Never know when I may need the upper hand," he said with a smirk.

"I'll make you a deal. If you promise to keep this to yourself, we'll bring my guys out here and see how they handle it. You may end up with a few dead turkeys but it'll be pretty damn funny."

"All right. My lips are sealed."

"Phew," Jay joked, while wiping his forehead with the back of his hand. "So is this one of the regular pranks played at AllSport?"

"Yeah, it humbles even the toughest of athletes," Reid said. "Then after they show their true colors, whenever they get a little too cocky, the people around them start making gobbling noises. It really pisses them off most of the time."

"I better not hear any gobbling. I don't get pissed off, I just get even."

Reid and Buck "Oooohed," in unison and Buck held up trembling hands in mock fright.

"OK, OK, enough nonsense for one night. Let's go. I need to get to sleep."

As they continued their walk, Jay was wide-eyed and seemed to be watching all directions at once.

They arrived at Reid and Buck's house on the grounds.

"Can I borrow your golf cart to go to my suite?" Jay asked.

"No need," Buck said. "All your stuff is here. We figured we'd be spending a lot of time together during the investigation so you might as well stay in the house with us. It's quieter than your usual suite and a lot nicer."

"A little quiet would be nice. Thanks."

7

The house was a classic colonial, very big without being ostentatious. Buck and Reid each had their own wing with bedroom, sitting room, and office. A state-of-the-art kitchen allowed Reid to fulfill his latent desire of being a gourmet chef. Buck couldn't cook; he felt accomplished making scrambled eggs. "Eating in" usually meant having a meal delivered from The Winner's Circle or Champs, the other campus restaurant. There was a large dining room, a library that served as a smoking room, and two guest bedrooms. In the basement were a theater that sat twenty comfortably and a small gym. The campus housing maid service cleaned the house daily.

• • •

Before retiring, Jay called the night receptionist to request a five a.m. wake-up call.

Buck and Reid sat in the library. Reid flipped back and forth between ESPN, the Food Network, and The Golf Channel.

"Dammit Reid, will you stop changing channels. You're making my head spin. I don't care what we watch, just pick a channel and leave it."

Reid tossed the clicker to Buck and said, "Here, I'm not really watching anyway."

"Why don't you go hit the sack?"

"'Cause I'd just lie there and think too much. I can't believe he's gone, Buck. We had tickets for the opera tonight. The girls were supposed to meet us at Lincoln Center. Speaking of them, I should call Shane to see how Karen is doing. I can't believe Jay is sending someone to check her out. The shit is gonna fly when she finds out she's a suspect. They don't know who their dealing with. I wouldn't want to be there, that's for sure. Did you ever see her when she gets mad?"

"No, why?"

"Well, let's just say you wouldn't want to be within throwing distance, and she's got a good arm." Reid got up and said, "I'll be right back."

"Tell her I said hello," Buck said while picking up the remote. He flipped through the channels and stopped just in time to catch the tail end of the eleven o'clock news. What he saw snapped him to attention. It was his interview with Linda Caruso. "*Damn,*" he thought, "*I've got to lose a few pounds.*" When his interview was over, another came on. It was another reporter from the same station interviewing a guy at AllSport housing. It was a young baseball player in training. Buck yelled loudly, "What the hell is this guy doing? Who does he think he is?" Reid came running in to see what the problem was. Jay's door opened and Jay came groggily out of his room.

"What are you yelling about, Buck? I'm trying to sleep."

"Take a look for yourself."

The guy on TV was in the middle of a statement. "Yeah, All-Sport is cool. It gives ball players like me a chance at the big league. I mean, I probably would have made it anyway, but AllSport pretty much guarantees it. Big league, big contracts, big endorsements, *everything,* man."

"Have things changed here on campus since Bob Thomas's

death?" the reporter asked.

"Well, security has always been tight around here. At least since Reid Clark's death threats, it has. But now it's like a jail, man. You can't go anywhere without a security guard or cop in your face. Hey, by the way, isn't there supposed to be a guard with you? Every other reporter has a guard with them."

The three men were staring at the screen in disbelief. "I guess he didn't take our discussion at the meeting too seriously. Do either of you know him?" Jay asked.

"Yeah, everyone here knows him," Reid said. "He's Dwayne Williams, a baseball player. He's good. He would have gone pro. It's a shame he's got a big mouth. He just bought himself a ticket outta here. We'll send him home tomorrow. What an idiot!"

"Well, I'm going back to sleep. Buck, if there are any more surprises on TV, please wait till the morning to let me know."

"Sorry," Buck apologized.

Buck turned back to the TV. "Shall we see if any of our other rocket scientists shot off their mouths on camera?" He flipped through the channels watching each news station for a couple of minutes. Sure enough, channel five had another athlete rambling on about the day's events. This time it was a woman speed skater.

"Yeah, I was running early this morning and saw a van right about where the body was found. I noticed it because the only vehicles you ever see around here are white golf carts or white maintenance trucks, all with the AllSport logo on them. The van didn't belong there, but I didn't think about it till I heard about the murder."

"Shit!" Buck yelled loudly. He walked over to the kitchen counter to get his radio and paged Al.

Jay dragged himself out of his room once again. "What now?"

Reid explained as Buck radioed Al to bring the girl over immediately.

"Well, you may have some idiots on campus, but at least this one might be helpful. It's time to offer some reward money. It should help jog some people's memory and, *of course,* make some others lie. Let's start by offering ten grand. That oughta raise some interest around here. My interviewing team is meeting me at the heliport in the morning when I land. They'll take the chopper back up here and be ready to start the interviews by lunchtime. I want them interviewing everyone on campus over the next few days. Buck, can you set up some kind of schedule and inform everyone that it's important for them to be on time? Can you also put the reward on the campus closed circuit TV system?"

"Sure, I'll get it done first thing in the morning. I'll do the reward broadcast myself. Ten thousand for any information that helps lead to an arrest. Right?"

"Exactly. Do me a favor. When you make the announcement, mention that anyone found to be giving false information will be asked to leave AllSport permanently. Otherwise we're gonna have a never-ending line of worthless interviews."

"Good idea."

There was a knock at the front door. Reid yelled, "Come in, it's unlocked."

"No, it's not," Jay said. "I locked it before I went to sleep the first time. You both need to tighten up your own security until we know who did this. In fact, I want to talk to you more about that later."

"Fine by me," Reid said as he walked toward the door and let in Al with a tall, blond, muscular woman dressed in an AllSport warm-up suit.

"Reid, this is Melanie Hundt," Al said.

"Just Mel, please," she corrected him.

"Mel, please come over and sit down. We need to discuss some things." They walked over and Reid introduced her to Jay and

Buck. "Sit down right here, Mel," Reid pointed to a chair across from where Jay was sitting on the couch. She sat and fidgeted nervously.

"Mel, would you like something to drink?" Jay asked trying to put her at ease.

"No thanks, I'm OK."

"All right, then please tell us what you saw this morning."

"Well, I run early every morning. I change my route around campus every day because otherwise it gets really boring. This morning as I was passing the basketball dome I noticed a van parked near the corner. I only noticed it because you never see any vehicles on campus other than the white AllSport maintenance vehicles."

"Can you describe the van?" Jay asked.

"Sure, it was dark blue. It was parked with its rear backed up to the edge of the garden. The back doors were open when I passed it, and I saw movement behind the van through the windshield. I figured it was a gardener or something. I didn't think twice about it until the meeting this morning."

"Did you notice the make or model of the van?"

"No."

"Did you see if there was more than one person behind the van?"

"Didn't really look."

"Can you describe any clothing? Any colors, anything at all? Think hard, Mel."

"No, not really. Sorry."

"Mel, you said you saw movement. What did you see? A head, an arm, what? I need you to think really hard. You had to see hair color, clothing, something. Close your eyes and try to picture what you saw."

Mel looked up and closed her eyes for a minute. She broke the silence, saying, "Dark…dark hair…and a light green shirt, like the color of hospital clothes. Wait a minute, I remember noise coming from the van like someone was inside and there was movement behind it at the same time. There must have been more than one person."

"Good, Mel. Keep going. What else do you see?"

She kept her eyes closed for another few seconds before slowly shaking her head. "That's it, nothing else. I kept running, and I can't even believe I saw everything I just described. I'm usually in the zone when I'm running. My mind is elsewhere so I don't pay attention to the pain. Seeing the van was a temporary distraction, but I really didn't give it any more thought. I certainly didn't know how important it was till now."

"You have been a big help. Thanks," Jay said.

"Mel, I'm afraid I have to ask why you spoke to the reporter before coming to us?" Buck asked. "You were at the meeting this morning. I know I was very clear about not speaking with the press. You intentionally disregarded my request. I need to understand why."

Mel lowered her head, "I'm sorry, Mr. Green. I know it was wrong but I couldn't help myself. You see, my sport is not one of the more glamorous high-paying sports. If I'm fast enough, I'll qualify for the Olympics. If I'm fast enough at the Olympics, then I'll medal. Then what? Tell me, how many skaters do you represent?"

Buck shook his head. "None."

"Exactly. In fact, I'll bet between the three of you, you can't name more than a handful of speed skaters who have become financially successful by skating. It just doesn't happen. I skate for the love of skating. I feel extremely lucky to be an AllSport athlete. But my expectations for any kind of monetary rewards are slim to none. This was the first time a news reporter ever wanted my view on anything. Although I knew it was wrong, I was overcome with desire for a moment of fame. I made the wrong decision. What else can I say? I'm sorry."

"You've put me in a terrible spot," Buck said. "I understand everything you've explained and I never realized it before. It has to be difficult to see the fame and fortune that other athletes stand to gain from their sport. Not many speed skaters make the headlines or the big money. Only a few come to mind like Apolo Ohno or Dan Jansen or Bonnie Blair. I can think of a few others but you're right, not many. I've got a big problem, though, Mel, and I don't feel good about this but you can't stay at AllSport. If I let you stay it sends a bad message to the entire campus. We'll lose control of all the athletes with the media. Where do you live?"

"Wisconsin."

"Where do you train at home?"

"At The Pettit National Ice Center."

"I'll tell you what. You have about a year until the Olympic Trials. If you make the Team, then you will be training with them. ICSF will cover your living and training expenses until then. Mel, I'm doing this because I really believe you meant no harm to the investigation or to AllSport. But if word of this arrangement gets out, I will be very unhappy and the financial support will cease. You will be leaving campus tomorrow. We will fly you home. I want you to join a local gym. Your training regiment is to remain exactly as if you were here. You'll need a fax machine. We will create a form for you to fill out and send us weekly. Who is your trainer here at camp?"

"Sue Sweeney."

"OK, I'll have Sue determine your schedule and your diet. Who was your coach at home?"

"My dad. He still competes regularly."

"Good. We'll cover your living and skating expenses. If your father can commit the time, we will pay him on a consulting basis. I will speak with him myself first thing tomorrow to explain everything. I'll want his signature on a weekly form confirming your workouts and weigh-ins and diet.

"Mel, I know this sounds pretty strict but I think I'm being very reasonable. You really blew it today. One more mistake and I will cut you off completely. Do you understand?"

She was crying by this point, but she got up, walked to Buck and hugged him saying a very teary "Yes, of course I understand. Thank you, Mr. Green, thank you so much."

"You're welcome. Now go back and start packing. You'll be leaving first thing in the morning. Thank you for the information and good luck with your training. I expect a medal from you in the Olympics."

"I'll do my best," she said with tears in her eyes. She gave him another quick hug, said goodbye to the others, and left.

"Look who's getting soft," Reid kidded.

"I like her. Seems like a good kid."

"I agree."

Jay was already on the phone with the on-duty officer at the police station. "Sergeant, I need a 'BOLO' for a dark blue van. We're looking for one or two suspects. Only description so far is dark hair and light green shirt or coat. Assume they are armed and dangerous."

The sergeant had obviously questioned Jay's authority. Jay's next words were stinging. "No problem, Sergeant," he seethed, "I will be happy to call and wake your chief right now. I hope you enjoyed your career because once Dave hears about this, you're through."

After a moment of silence Jay said, "Smart move, Sergeant. Yes, they've been on the road since early this morning." He looked at his watch and winced. "I mean yesterday morning. They could be anywhere. Take down my cell number and call me as soon as you hear anything." He gave his number, then finished the call saying, "And, Sergeant, Chief Wheeler will not hear anything from me about your attitude, but I'll tell you what, a little mutual respect will help our relationship in the future." He listened and then said, "No problem, Sergeant, good night."

Jay hung up, shook his head, and rolled his eyes. "Another bone-head cop. I should be used to it by now, but it always gets to me. There's always a few that get their feathers ruffled when I take over their cases. They try to stand up to me until I put them in their place. Then I have to calm them down so the animosity doesn't spread through the department. It's the same every time. Oh well, I guess it comes with the turf."

"The price you pay as the new sheriff in town, huh?" Buck asked.

"Yeah, something like that," he sighed.

"Hey, what's a bolo?" Reid asked.

"Be on the lookout. Same as an APB...Oh, by the way, I have Joel and Stu coming up after they follow their leads. I also have two other guys on the way. I want both of you to have round-the-clock protection. I want no argument on this, OK?"

Reid and Buck looked at each other and nodded their acceptance.

As Jay got up he said, "If I don't get some sleep I'm going to be worthless tomorrow. Good night, for the last time, I hope. Buck, do me a favor, turn off the TV!"

Buck and Reid snickered as Jay went back to bed.

"I hate having bodyguards around all the time," Reid muttered.

"Yeah, me too, but it's a lot better than getting shot."

"Hate to be negative but they didn't help me too much last time. Did they?"

"You were an open target on the putting green. Nobody could have stopped that bullet."

"Yeah, I guess. Well, I'm beat, I'm going to hit the sack. See you in the morning."

8

Jody Macintire stopped at the gates in front of the Thomas mansion. She took her hands off the steering wheel, clasped them together and pushed them out in front of her, palms forward, cracking her knuckles. She took a deep breath and let it out slowly, mentally preparing herself for her upcoming investigation. The home was perched atop a magnificent acre and a half that gently sloped down to the waters of Long Island's North Shore. The manicured property was itself worth a fortune. With the house, the value was well over five million. Jody drove through the gates and noticed surveillance cameras peeking from trees that lined the long winding driveway. Eventually she arrived in front of a grand colonial with three-story pillars on the front porch. A large black Mercedes and a black Hummer H2 were parked off to the side. Jody parked her Jeep Wrangler next to the Hummer. She couldn't help but look inside the dark shaded windows as she walked past. She shrugged her shoulders and thought, *Pretty cool if you own an oil refinery.*

She walked up the stone steps to the front porch. The massive, wooden front door resembled the entrance to a cathedral. It was about ten feet tall and five feet wide with a rounded top and a large lead-paned stained glass window. She looked for a doorbell but there was none. Her gaze fell upon a knocker in the center of the door so big it looked too heavy for one hand. *You've got to be kidding*, she thought. She lifted the knocker and let it fall, once, then again. She laughed to herself; the noise was loud enough that she figured the neighbors were probably answering their doors right now. She waited patiently for about a minute. As she reached for the knocker to try again the door slowly opened. A beautiful woman standing in the doorway said, "You must be Jody."

"I am so sorry about your husband, Mrs. Thomas."

"No, Jody, I'm Shane Clark. Karen is inside lying down. Please come in. Would you like something to drink? Coffee, tea?"

"Coffee would be fine, thank you."

"Follow me. We'll be more comfortable in the den." Jody followed her down the hallway past the living and dining rooms. A peek into the elegant dining room revealed vaulted ceilings and a highly polished black-lacquered table with seating for about twenty. Shane showed her into the den and offered her a seat on one of the oversized red leather couches. "Let me go get Karen. I just want to warn you, she looks terrible. In spite of her medication, she barely slept a wink last night."

"I'm sure. This must be such a horrible thing to endure." Jody was concentrating on how she would tactfully press Karen for information and check out her alibi without creating an uproar. It was not going to be easy. Jody looked around the room. Next to the floor-to-ceiling stone hearth fireplace was a full-sized drop-down movie screen. Magnificent pastel paintings filled any open wall space. The wall overlooking the backyard was mostly glass, revealing a mesmerizing view of Long Island Sound.

Karen entered the room wearing a bulky thigh length off-white sweater and black leggings. Red puffy eyes and a runny nose were surrounded by a tangled mess of brown hair. She walked over to Jody, who stood, shook hands and introduced herself. Karen sat on the couch opposite Jody and tucked her bare feet under her.

"Please accept my condolences, Karen. I know this is a very difficult time and I hate to bother you, but the faster we get information, the faster we can find whoever did this."

"I understand," Karen said between sniffles.

"Do you need a moment or may I start asking questions?"

"Go ahead, ask away."

"First, can you think of anyone who Bob had any problems with? Business, personal, anyone at all?"

She thought for a moment, then shrugged her shoulders. "He always had arguments on the phone. It was just the way he did business."

"Was he very confrontational?"

"Yeah, with just about everyone, except Reid, me included."

"You?"

"Hell, yes," she said with a wicked laugh. "We fought all the time."

"How were you two getting along lately?"

"Same as usual, but our relationship changed after his affair. Oh, what am I saying? You don't need to hear this crap."

"Karen, I really do. The more you tell me, the better."

"Can't this wait?" she sobbed.

"I'm sorry, I know this is difficult but it's important that we discuss it now."

"All right." She dabbed her eyes with a tissue.

"Please tell me about the affair."

"It was a little over a year ago. I went up to AllSport to surprise him. I got to the house and the surprise was on me. In retrospect, it was kind of funny. Not at the time, though, because I sort of lost my cool."

"I'll bet."

"I actually caught them in the bedroom. After yelling at them, I started throwing things. In fact, I threw almost everything in that room that wasn't nailed down. Books, lamps, shoes, everything." She giggled a little. "The bitch rolled off the side of the bed to hide from me. I'm sure she thought I was insane. I probably was at the moment. I just kept throwing things and cursing. She did her best to throw some clothes on but eventually gave up and ran out of the room. I think she fell down the steps." Another giggle.

"She was trying to put her pants on before leaving. But I threw one last book at her and she ran. She finally got out the front door with just her panties and bra on." Karen was laughing by this point. Picturing the whole scenario, Shane and Jody couldn't help but laugh as well. As their laughter subsided, Karen said, "I've never described that scene to anyone. That actually felt pretty good." Then she began to cry again. Between sobs she said, "I really did love the jerk." Shane walked over and gave her a hug.

Jody excused herself to use the ladies room.

"It's on the right as you walk into the hallway," Shane explained.

Jody had driven two and a half hours from New Jersey and had filled her enormous travel coffee mug twice during the trip. Then another cup when she arrived. The Java had been essential after spending half the night researching Bob Thomas on the Internet then peeling her eyes open at five-thirty in order to get here on time. The laughing episode created enough pressure on her bladder that she needed the restroom quickly. Karen needed the break anyway.

While in the bathroom, Jody thought about the interview. It was going better than she would have expected. Karen was openly revealing things that Jody thought she would have to pry out of her. She thought about how to continue from where they left off. She wanted to hear if Karen would mention the demands she had placed on Bob in order to continue their marriage. An open admission would certainly lead one to believe her innocence, yet Jody would still need to pursue her investigation. She washed up, checked herself in the mirror, and went back to the den.

Shane called out from the kitchen, "Jody, how about something to eat or drink? I'm toasting bagels for Karen and me. Would you like one?"

"Sure, thank you."

"And some more coffee?"

"No, thanks, but some water would be great. Can I help you?"

"No, I've got it, thanks."

Jody sat back down across from Karen.

"I'm sorry, Jody," Karen said.

"*Sorry*? Don't be ridiculous. I think you're doing very well, considering."

"I guess."

"Let me know when you're ready to continue."

Karen took a deep breath and slowly let it out, "Go ahead, I'll be all right."

"OK, tell me what happened after the confrontation."

"Well, after she left, I went back into the bedroom and continued yelling. I called him every name in the book. Then I told him we were done and I just left. My ride home seemed like it took forever. I cried the entire way. He must have called my cell ten times but I wouldn't answer. I didn't talk to him for two days. He called and spoke with the girls and tried to get them to hand me the phone. I would take the phone and just hit the off button. It was tough, especially when the girls begged me to talk to him. When I finally did, he apologized endlessly and pleaded to see me so we could talk. He told me he loved me more than he had realized and had made a huge mistake. He said he would do anything to stay together. I told him I'd think about it then hung up on him. Later, I spoke with a friend who had gone through the same thing. Her attorney had offered her a solution that almost guaranteed her husband would keep his dick in his pants instead of another woman."

Jody's eyes widened with surprise. "How could he guarantee that?"

"It was a fairly simple solution. If Bob wanted to come back, he would have to sign an agreement. If he had another affair, one-night-stand, or even touched another woman, he would lose everything in a quick divorce. I would get both homes, the cars, the boat, and all the money."

"Wow, harsh but simple."

"Yeah, I guess he really loved me or maybe it was just easier than going through a messy divorce and losing everything anyway."

"How were things afterwards?"

"They actually got much better. In fact, the last year was the best of our entire marriage. He spent a lot of time with the girls and me when they were home from school. He doted on me excessively, lots of flowers, presents, and spontaneous weekends away. It was nice." Tears had welled up in her eyes while she was speaking. Now the floodgates opened again.

Shane had joined them while Karen had been talking. Jody stood and motioned for Shane to come with her. They walked over to the kitchen. "I want to give her a break for a little while," Jody said. "Why don't you suggest we take a walk? It's a beautiful day and she could probably use the fresh air."

"You're right, I think that would be good for her. Let me talk to her."

"I'm going to make a quick call while you get her ready."

"All right, the phone is over there." Shane pointed.

"I'll just use my cell, thanks."

Shane walked out of the room. Jody stepped outside on the front porch and dialed Jay.

"Hello," Jay answered.

"Hey, it's me."

"How's it going?"

"Better than expected. She's running at the mouth, seems genuinely distraught. I'm about to finish up. I want to see if she talks about the insurance policy. How are *you* doing?"

"A little tired but OK. I'm on my way up to Westchester now. Turns out that Riley's wife took him back after he begged long enough. I spent the last two hours going over things at his old company on Wall Street."

"Find anything worthwhile?"

"Well, he isn't very well liked by his old partners. I guess that what happens when you steal twelve million dollars from people."

"That's a significant number."

"Nah, down here that's play money. Let me call you back a little later. They just brought my car up from the garage."

"OK, talk to you later."

"Bye."

9

Despite the typically frustrating New York traffic, Jay's drive up to Westchester was easy. He arrived at Riley's house in Purchase in half an hour. Jay had been to the area on many occasions, usually to play golf with a client. There were almost as many country clubs in the area as homes. It seemed one of the necessities for wealthy golfers is to live near their golf club. If you were rich enough to own one of the estates in the area, you had your choice of upscale clubs. Riley's estate was adjacent to one of the most prestigious. As Jay pulled up to the front gates on Purchase Street, he rehearsed in his mind what he would say to gain entrance.

He pulled up to the intercom box and was about to push the button when a woman's voice asked, "May I help you?"

An automatic device had probably been tripped that rang or buzzed in the house informing them of arriving visitors. "Yes, please, I'm Investigator Scott. I need to speak with Mr. Riley."

"May I see your ID and Badge, Mr. Scott?" she said in a slightly irritated voice.

"See it?"

"Just hold it up facing the intercom box."

Jay was annoyed that he didn't notice the covert camera lens in the intercom box pointing right at him. He held up his ID and an old police badge that he used in instances like this.

"Thank you, officer. May I ask why you need to speak with my husband? He's a very busy man."

"Ma'am, I need to ask him a few questions. Someone he knew through business was murdered yesterday, and we are following up any past relationships."

"Murdered," she gasped. "Who was murdered and why would Edwin know anything about it?"

"Ma'am, if you'll let me in, I'll explain it all face to face."

"Give me a minute, please."

Jay sat there for about two minutes and was about to push the intercom button again when the gates started to swing open. "Come in, Officer."

"Thank you," he said as he drove through the massive stone pillars and iron gates. The driveway snaked through an immaculately kept front yard with tremendous randomly placed metal sculptures. The final turn in the driveway revealed a medieval-looking stone mansion. Jay had been to many large homes but none like this. It was breathtaking. The lawn next to the house had not one, but two putting greens on it, about one hundred yards apart. The far green even had a couple of bunkers flanking it. Jay scanned the property and, sure enough, there was a tee box next to the house. Jay had to laugh; living next to a golf course wasn't enough for this guy. He needed his own private practice holes. *Amazing*, thought Jay, shaking his head as he walked to the front door and rang the bell.

"Just a minute," came a voice through the intercom.

After a long wait, the door finally opened. "Good day, sir," said a well-dressed man who Jay figured must be the butler. "Please come in and follow me." They walked down a hallway to two large, beautifully grained, mahogany, French doors. The butler dramatically opened both doors simultaneously. "Please make yourself comfortable. The Rileys will join you shortly. May I get you a drink or a nibble, sir?"

"Coffee, thank you," said Jay, thinking, *A nibble, what am I, a hamster?*

Jay entered and looked around. The room was furnished with leather couches and chairs. Books filled every inch of the floor-to-ceiling bookshelves that lined the dark paneled walls. A rolling ladder rested at the end of its track, near the far wall. A polished, walnut wet-bar with a brass draft beer tower stood in one corner and a card table with six chairs filled another. A faint aroma of leather, cigars, and cognac helped create a very comfortable, relaxed atmosphere. Jay walked over and gazed at the seemingly endless rows of books. You could learn a lot about people from the books they read. The collection was one any avid reader would envy.

Jay was a chain reader. He preferred mysteries, but he read everything he could get his hands on. He planned to write his own book after he retired. He kept a notebook that he updated after solving each of his cases. He knew the stories had bestseller potential; he only hoped his writing could pass muster.

He always felt good browsing bookshelves. He had read quite a few of the books. There was a wide array of mystery, action, and romance. Other shelves were dedicated to business, religion, spiritualism, and history. He found a collection of instructional books on golf. He was studying another row when a topic caught his attention. An entire shelf was dedicated to books about firearms, hunting, and target shooting. A few titles containing the word "sniper" were sandwiched in as well. *Interesting,* he thought. As he moved on, studying the room, the butler walked in with Jay's coffee. He set the silver tray on the coffee table and asked, "Will that be all, sir?"

"Yes, thank you very much." Jay felt uncomfortable being served as if he were royalty. He walked over and sank into a luxuriously soft, chocolate-brown, leather armchair. It practically swallowed him. He dared not sit back in this chair; he'd doze off in minutes. He leaned forward and, after fixing his coffee, viewed the magazine collection on the table: *Golf Digest, Cigar Aficionado, Wine Enthusiast, Gun World, Guns & Ammo, Handguns, Field & Stream, Shooting Sportsman, Rifle Shooter, Shooting Times, and Hunting*. He picked up *Rifle Shooter* and began leafing through it when Edwin Riley entered.

"I see you've made yourself comfortable," he said loudly. "Do you have an interest in riflery?"

"In fact I do." Jay stood and the two men approached each other and shook hands. "Hi, I'm Jay Scott."

"I'm quite sure there's no need for me to introduce myself. Now tell me what would the infamous Private Investigator, Mr. Jay Scott, want with li'l ol' me?"

Riley was big and obnoxiously loud. His rotund gut fell over his belt. He wore jeans and cowboy boots that were made from some exotic animal skin. The only thing missing was a ten-gallon Stetson, but then he was inside his own house so it was probably on a shelf somewhere. In fact when Jay looked closely he could see Riley's dark wavy hair was pressed down at the hat line. Unmistakable hat-head.

"Well, Mr. Riley…."

"Please call me Ed," Riley interrupted.

"Fine, Ed, you can call me Jay. The reason I'm here is to discuss Bob Thomas."

"Is that who was murdered? Couldn't have happened to a finer man," he said with a grin.

"Do I detect a hint of sarcasm? Did you harbor any ill feelings towards Bob?"

"Ill feelings my ass, Jay. Let's call a spade a spade. Maybe I was doing something a little wrong, but he blew the whistle and put me away for years. Am I supposed to like him?"

"Correct me if I'm wrong, Ed, but corporate theft to the tune of twelve million is more than a little wrong. Bob was only doing the job you and your partners hired him to do. In fact, I heard *you* were the one who hired him."

"We all make mistakes. Don't we?" Ed said with a smirk. "So tell me, Jay. What do you want from me? Don't tell me I'm a suspect."

Jay silently raised his brow.

"Ha, that's a good one." Ed let out a loud guffaw. "Look, I didn't like him much. In fact, I hated him, but I didn't kill him. How idiotic would that be? I just got out. You think I want to go back in. *No way, Jay.* One mistake was more than enough for me. This cowboy ain't gonna see the inside of another prison."

"Not a pleasant experience, huh?"

"Do you know what goes on behind bars? Of course you do. You know what they call someone like me? Scared straight, that's what. I will *never* break another law. Shit, I won't even drive my Ferrari over the speed limit."

"Ed, tell me, what have you been doing since you were released?"

"Playing golf, going to gun shows, shooting at my range, looking for business opportunities, mostly just staying out of trouble."

"Shooting at your range? What do you mean, *your* range?"

"Come with me, I'll show you."

Jay followed him out of the room and down the hall. They stopped in front of a large door. Ed punched a code into a keypad, turned a small key, and the door slid open, revealing an elevator. They stepped inside. Country music seemed to contradict the elaborate brass-detailed, mirrored walls. Jay noticed five buttons for different levels. Ed pressed a button labeled B2. The car started down and stopped at the sub-basement level. Ed opened a small access panel and pressed his entire hand on a horizontal pad with a window that was lit from below. Automatically, another panel opened at eye level and a device slid out that was similar to an eye exam machine. Ed stepped up and looked into the two eyepieces for a few seconds before stepping back. He turned to Jay who was looking at him with questioningly squinted eyes and his head slightly tilted.

"You can never be too safe, Jay. Door won't open without fingerprint and retina scan." A loud click was heard coming from the locking mechanism in the elevator door and Ed pushed it open to reveal a large room. Exotic guns lined the walls.

"Impressive," Jay remarked.

"Should be, it's the most valuable collection in the country."

Jay walked slowly around the room admiring the weapons. Handguns, rifles, shotguns, automatics, you name it, it was here. As Jay reached for a rifle, he asked, "You mind?"

"Be my guest."

The weapon Jay removed from the wall was a Tactical Operations—Bravo 51, the rifle of choice for many snipers. He lifted it to his shoulder and looked through the sight.

"That baby could take out a bumblebee from a hundred yards."

"I know, Ed," Jay said with some contempt.

"Wanna try it?"

"Sure."

As he followed Ed to one of three doors on the far wall he sniffed the chamber and the end of the barrel. The odor of gun cleaning fluid was overpowering. Obviously it was recently cleaned. Two full-sized rifles were carved into the door Ed opened.

"How often do you clean them all?" Jay asked.

"It's a full time job. Johnny has a cleaning schedule. He rotates the cleaning from one side of the room to the other. When he finishes the last gun, it's time to start again on the first." They walked through the door into the shooting range. Ed turned and walked to a room off to the side. "Hey, Johnny, I need a box of Federal Gold

Medal Match 175 shells and two headsets. Mr. Scott and I are gonna have a shoot-out."

Jay peeked over Ed's shoulder into the room. There were racks of ammo for every gun in the collection. In the center of the room a felt-lined tool bench was covered with rifle parts, cleaning solvents, lubricants, cleaning rags, and assorted brushes.

Johnny grabbed a box off a shelf and handed it to Ed. "Here you go. Are you going to shoot paper or video?"

"I'm gonna let Jay choose."

Jay followed Ed out to the two firing positions. "Take your pick, Jay. Would you prefer paper silhouettes or do you want to try video?"

"Why don't you show me video."

Ed pushed a few keys on a keyboard mounted to the wall. A menu came up on the color display above the keyboard offering what looked like different scenes. There were many options: Bullseye, Silhouette, Clay Pigeon-Trap, Clay Pigeon-Skeet, Deer, Turkey, Rabbit, Grouse, Bear, and Other.

"What's your choice?" Ed asked.

"What's 'other' stand for?"

"For when I get bored with animals," he said pushing the button with a grin. The next menu that came up showed: Bank Robber, Terrorist, Sniper, and Cowboy Shoot-Out.

"Interesting," Jay said.

"It's really no different than a kid's video game."

"I don't know too many kids who shoot live rounds for fun."

Ed laughed and said, "Tell you what. Shoot a few rounds at a video silhouette target and then we'll have a little contest between us. You game?"

Ed pressed a button and a silhouette target showed up on video at the far end of Range One. He handed Jay the box of ammunition and a headset. Jay opened the bolt and slid a round into the chamber. He put on the headset, as did Ed, then lifted the gun to his shoulder and aimed.

Just as he was pulling the trigger, Ed said, "You might want to rest it on the supports; gives the truest sniper feel."

Jay fired as he was. Ed turned to look at the wall display; it showed accuracy points up to one hundred. At the distance Jay was shooting, anything over ninety was exceptional. In fact, the best Ed had ever scored was ninety-six, and that was in the prone position. A good standing score was eighty or better. Ed's jaw dropped. The screen displayed ninety-nine.

"Damn, I'd say beginner's luck, but I think I know better."

Jay chambered another round, lifted the gun, and fired. They both turned to look; ninety-eight.

"All right, let's forget about our shoot-out. Where the hell did you learn to shoot like that?"

"FBI SWAT."

"You think I could sign up for a lesson or two?" Ed said with a chuckle.

"Not likely." Jay chambered and fired one more shot. Ninety-nine again.

"Damn, the boys'll never believe this. You may have to come back to prove it to them."

"*The boys*?"

"Couple of guys from the club. They come over to shoot once a week after golf. Hey, how about a cigar? Got some great Cohibas. We can go out and hit a few golf balls while we're talkin'."

"Sounds good. Before we go, can I take a quick look at some of the target scenes on the video system?"

"Which ones?"

"How about sniper?"

Ed pushed the button and the screen came alive. A voice came through Jay's headset and a typed description on the screen read:

Sniper Simulation: You are NYPD SWAT, your target is an armed robber in a brownstone on eightieth street. He has two hostages. Good Luck!

The following image gave Jay a view as if he was on the street, getting orders from his SWAT team commander. His instructions were to get to the rooftop on the building across the street and set up for a clean shot as quickly as possible, in case the negotiator failed. As soon as the commander yelled go, a digital stopwatch started ticking off seconds in the corner of the screen.

Jay removed the headset and said, "OK, let's go smoke those cigars."

"Don't you want to take out the bad guy?"

"No, thanks," said Jay, thinking, *that's exactly why I'm here, schmuck*. "Tell me, Ed, how did you get your hands on this stuff? That video is not for sale to the public. It's sniper training for law enforcement. And the guns, what can I say? Most of them could get you another few years in the joint."

"Come on. You can get anything you want these days. The internet is like a black market department store."

"I thought you said you weren't breaking the law ever again?"

"Oh, gimme a break. Look, none of this collection ever leaves these rooms. I don't bring any of it to shows or outdoor ranges or anywhere for that matter."

"Right," Jay said in disbelief.

"Look, I don't give a damn what you believe; I'm telling you the truth."

Jay nodded. "Let's just go get those cigars."

"Good idea." Ed returned the unused portion of the ammo and the rifle to Johnny and they walked out. Jay took one more look around the room as he walked over to the second door. There was a bowling ball and ten pins carved into it. He opened the door and saw two lanes and a small bar. He let the door close and walked to the last door on which a set of golf clubs was carved in a fan shape. He looked at Ed who nodded and said, "Fully computerized driving range with video of all the best courses in the world. You can play a full round at Pebble Beach, Augusta National, St. Andrews, almost anywhere you want. Come on, let's go up."

Jay followed Ed into the elevator, and they rode up to the main floor and walked back to the library. Ed opened a side door and they entered a small walk-in humidor.

"Take three of whatever you enjoy. I recommend these." He picked up a few Cohiba Double Coronas Edicion 2003's. "Or these," he said, pointing to the Cohiba Piramide Edicion 2001's. "I can only get these once in a while. They just arrived yesterday and they're marvelous."

"Whatever you're smoking works for me," Jay said.

They each cut and lit their cigars and left the humidor. "Wanna beer?" Ed asked as he opened a refrigerator door that simulated its adjacent wood cabinets. He grabbed himself a couple of Heinekens. "I'd pour you a fresh draft but these are easier to carry outside."

Jay opted for a Diet Coke, then followed Ed to a door at the end of yet another hallway. Ed opened it and they walked down a few steps to the marble floor of the garage which was more like a showroom of fine automobiles. They walked past a Ferrari Enzo, a Lamborghini Murcielago R-GT, a Porsche Carrera GT, a Hummer H2, and two Harley Davidson 100th Anniversary Fatboys. A glimpse at the other side of the garage revealed a convertible Bentley and a stretch Mercedes. Each vehicle was polished to a high luster. Last but not least was a custom golf cart with two bags of clubs strapped on in the back. Ed sat in the driver's seat and patted the seat next to him. "Sit down. Take a load off." Jay sat and Ed pushed the button on the remote garage door opener. They drove out and around the house to one of two elevated tee boxes.

"So tell me, I can guess the approximate value of the gun collection, but how about the cars?"

"A few mill. The Ferrari and Lamborghini are worth over a million together."

"Ed, I have to ask two questions. Obviously you've got plenty of money. Where did it all come from and why would you steal a measly twelve million if you really didn't need it?"

"Question one is easy, my great grandfather was a scientist. He helped invent what became a widely used form of antibiotic."

Ed nodded.

"Question two is a little more difficult to answer. You see, my firm made a lot of money. Therefore, I got paid well, big salary, bigger bonuses. This is gonna sound ridiculous but it all got too easy. There was no spark in my life, no excitement. I started to play options and did it all on margin accounts. Obviously not because I had to, it was just more exciting. Anyway, my decisions were not good and I got a few margin calls. They were no problem, I just wrote the checks, but it was exciting, I got kinda hooked. Next thing I knew, I was getting a rush from losing money. Sounds absurd now, even to me. Well, it got worse, because I started dreaming that I lost it all. I mean *everything*. It got to the point that I couldn't sleep. So how did I solve the problem? I started writing company checks to cover my margin calls. Not too smart, huh?" He gave Jay a dumb look.

"No, not really."

"Well, the rest is history. Got caught. Did time. Now I'm out and I'm a lot smarter. You know you can learn a lot from your mistakes, but you can learn even more from the really dumb ones."

"Yeah, I've made my share."

"Why don't you tee one up? The closer green is about a hundred yards, the far one is about two hundred."

Jay pulled out a three wood and reached for a few balls and

tees. He noticed the balls were Eagle's Freeze. He held one up and said, "You know Reid Clark endorses these."

"Yeah, I've seen him in all their ads. Heard his endorsement contract was close to one hundred million. Why did you mention him?"

"He and Bob were very close friends and Bob was CFO at AllSport. You know about AllSport and the ICSF, don't you?"

"Do I know about it?" Ed said as he held up his right hand and wiggled his pinkie. "You know what it takes to get one of these babies, don't you?"

Jay studied the ring. "That's platinum, isn't it?"

"Sure is."

"You get that for a million dollar donation, right?"

"Try five…Big bucks, right? But I'll tell you what; it's the best damn charity in this country. I mean, giving money to help fight cancer and diabetes and sick kids is great; in fact I give to them all, but the ICSF is a gem. Think of all the good it does. It gets inner-city kids off the street. It keeps them out of jail and off drugs. It increases the country's chances for medals in the Olympics. It raises the level of competition in professional sports. And above and beyond all that, I get a tax break and a nice ring. No other charity I know helps at so many levels. It's brilliant."

Jay's curiosity got the better of him, "Excuse me for being direct, but how much money do you have?"

"Almost half a billion. It's more than I'll ever need and my portfolio just keeps growing."

"Must be nice." Jay took a few practice swings before stepping up and hitting the ball that he had teed up. He hit a wicked slice and said with a laugh, "Good thing you don't have close neighbors." He teed up another and hit a nice shot, just short of a bunker in front of the green. "That's better."

Ed hit his five-wood, sending the ball a few yards short of the green. He smiled as it rolled onto the dance floor, pin-high.

"Nice shot," Jay said as he started walking.

Ed jumped into the cart and drove up next to him. "Hop in."

"Did you ever think that maybe a little exercise might be good for you?" Jay asked.

"Ha! Yeah, *me exercise*? Drinking beer and smoking a cigar are practically manual labor to me."

Jay couldn't help from laughing as he sat down next to Ed. "That was very funny."

"Right, about as funny as a heart attack."

Jay let out another chuckle.

They finished out the hole and chipped to the other green. After they both sank their putts, Jay said, "Thanks Ed, it's time for me to go. I'll be in touch."

Ed drove him to his car. "So, am I still a suspect?"

"I'll be in touch."

"I'm tellin' you, Jay, you're wastin' your time with me. I had nothin' to do with it."

"Hope not."

Jay drove down the driveway and turned right toward Westchester Airport. It was only a couple of minutes away and the chopper was waiting for him. He grabbed his cell and dialed Jody. She answered on the third ring. "Hi, anything new?" he asked.

"Yeah, she's clear. I'm sure of it. She told me all about the insurance policy. I didn't even have to ask. Where do you want me next?"

"Meet me at the heliport on the East Side near the WaterClub. I just left Riley. I'll fill you in when I see you. Park your car someplace long-term since I don't know when we'll get back. I want to head back to AllSport. Have you heard from Leigh or Emma?"

"No, not yet."

"OK, see you soon." Jay ended the call, then found Joel's number and dialed. Hearing Joel's voicemail message, he hung up.

10

Joel and Stu had been on the streets of L.A. on Faxton's turf for a few hours. As it turned out, Faxton had been released from jail about eight months after his fight at AllSport. Joel had already contacted the chief at the local precinct, who told him that Faxton had been arrested again. The bust had only occurred two weeks prior and was the result of a street basketball game that ended in a gang fight. Faxton was only charged with disturbing the peace, so he was back on the street that night. After questioning a local bodega owner of the gang's whereabouts, they were told about an abandoned building down a back alley that had become the Judges' "crib." Word of Joel and Stu's search had quickly spread to the gang. As they made their way down the alley it became apparent that the Judges had been tipped off. Two guys were walking slowly toward them. A rapid turn of the head confirmed that two more were coming up behind them. They were obviously sent out on a fact-finding mission because no weapons were drawn. As they closed in, Joel raised his hands over his head and said, "We're only looking for information, not a fight."

"What ya wanna know?" slurred a guy with a shaved head and a scar on his left cheek.

"We need to speak with Bill Faxton."

"Who da fuck you think you are? You tellin' me what you

neeeed. Like I giva shit. Tell ya what. Turn around now, walk away, and you'll live to see tomorrow."

Joel and Stu glanced at each other but didn't move.

"I *said* get the fuck outta here, now."

Stu just smiled.

"You think I'm funny? Dumb fucks, now you're gonna die."

Within minutes, three of the thugs were down and unconscious. The one remaining guy was huge. Before Stu could turn around, the guy slashed him with a seven-inch Recon Bowie knife. Joel spun and slammed his boot into the guy's head with a roundhouse kick. The guy's head snapped back, hitting the brick wall. Whatever drugs he was on sent him on a rampage. He yelled at the top of his lungs and charged Stu with his head down. Stu waited till he was close enough and, with perfect timing, jumped to the side and kicked up into the guy's throat while slamming his right fist on the back of his neck. The guy went down in a coughing fit and didn't get up. They both hurried to an open doorway where Joel ripped off Stu's torn sleeve and tied it tightly around his arm to slow the heavy bleeding. They ran to the end of the alley to the abandoned building.

Broken glass crunched under their feet as they entered. Every window was shattered. Remnants of small fires, ripped blankets, and old soiled mattresses were strewn about. Rats scampered over and around discarded, used hypodermic needles. The muffled thud of a bass speaker radiated from the bowels of the building. Joel and Stu followed the noise down two flights of stairs. They walked down a hallway, carefully scanning their surroundings. They were fairly sure that none of the guys that had attacked them in the alley had been able to inform the other gang members that they were approaching. Three were out cold and the big guy was barely conscious. The bandage around Stu's arm was already saturated with blood. He'd be all right for a while but needed stitches soon.

Both men had their automatics drawn and were inching toward the door from which the music was emanating. There had to be a lookout man in the building somewhere, unless that was the job of the four guys outside. They reached the door without any further surprises. The loud rap music made the next decision difficult. Usually they could decide how to enter an unknown situation based on what they heard through the door. They had a serious problem here. Enter with guns drawn and they'd create instant chaos and get nothing accomplished. Or enter with guns holstered and take the chance of getting shot. They looked at each other, each knowing what the other was thinking as they both frowned and shrugged. Stu put his gun away as Joel raised his into firing position. Each noticing the other's move caused them both to change their minds. Stu pulled his gun out and Joel holstered his. They both smiled; a little comic relief before you die can be good. Next thing they knew their decision was made for them as the door was opened by someone on the other side.

The room was dimly lit. The heavy chemical haze of burning drugs created an eerie atmosphere. A small group sat on filthy couches playing video games while passing a crack pipe. Two guys in the back of the room were huddled over a portable stove holding spoons over the flame. Looking closer at the table, Joel saw a small bag of syringes.

In the center of the room a guy and a girl were sprawled on a couch. The guy was looking at Joel and Stu as he laughed deep and loud. "You guys are fuckin' hilarious. Who you think you be? Andy and Barney from Mayberry? No, I got it; you're making the next Lethal Weapon movie. Come in, come in. I been waitin' for ya."

They stepped in carefully, each noticing guys in the front corners of the room with guns pointed at them. A quick glance at the wall behind them revealed a large flat-screen TV with surveillance video of different parts of the building. They gave each other a quick look, simultaneously shrugging their shoulders and raising their brows, each wondering how they could have missed the cameras.

"So tell me, what you wan wit Faxton? He fuck up again? Fuckin' guy just can't stay outta trouble. Always someone comin' round here lookin' for him. Gets ta be a fuckin' pain in my ass. I like my peace 'n quiet. I like to relax. Can't relax when guys like you are in my face lookin' for Faxton. I gotta hand it to you two, though, nobody ever got through the alley before. You guys are good. Take a look. The guys are still out cold." He hit a button on a keypad and a view of the alley popped up on the screen. "Wouldn't want to be you when they wake up." He laughed. "Oh, who my kiddin? You'd just kick their asses again. Right?"

"Right," Stu said. "Look, we're from AllSport, and we need to speak with him."

"He ain't here. Been gone for days. Tell me what it's about; I'll tell him when I see him."

"It's confidential," Joel said. "Do you know where we can find him?"

"I may lead the Judges, but I don't keep track of 'em. He could be anywhere, but he'll be back. Faxton always comes back. You gonna take him back to AllSport? You should. He'll go pro if you do. You ever see him play? Nobody 'round here can touch him. He's like a fuckin' magician with a basketball."

"Can you tell us where he lives or who he hangs out with?" Joel asked.

"He lives here. He hangs with Marco; they was joined at the hip till Faxton hooked up with his bitch, Wanda. He's got a problem now; Marco and Wanda hate each other."

"Where can I find them?"

"Marco's probably with him. The bitch? Go ask Carla. She's

over there with Net," he said, pointing to a guy and a girl across the room. "I think she lives with Wanda."

"Thanks for your help, man," Joel said.

"No problem. Let me ask you a question. What do you guys do at AllSport?"

"Recruiting and Martial Arts training."

"I figured, way you mothafuckers fight. It was beautiful, man. I ain't never seen nothin' like it. Tell ya what. I'll make ya'll a deal right now. I'll give you each ten large to teach my guys for a week."

"Thanks for the offer but we have a job to do already," Stu answered.

"Oh well. The offer stands if you change your mind."

"Great," Stu said. "We're gonna go talk to Carla, and then we're outta here."

Carla was snorting a line of something off a mirror as they approached. She looked up at Stu with sad puppydog eyes. In a sleepy, drug-induced voice, she asked, "Hey stud, want some H?"

"No thanks, Carla, but would you mind if we ask a few questions about your friend Wanda?"

She shrugged her shoulders and slurred, "Go 'head, ask away." Net was sitting next to her and attempted to open his eyes. He mumbled some unintelligible words before closing his eyes again.

Stu shook his head thinking, *the wonderful world of heroin. Why would anyone bother*? "Carla, where can I find Wanda? We need to talk to her."

She laughed lazily with eyes half closed. The heroin high was obviously kicking in. "Fuckifiknow," she slurred, barely moving her mouth. The words kind of spilled out.

"When did you see her last?" Stu asked with little hope of an answer.

Carla slumped over on Net. No response.

"She's fried. Let's get out of here," Joel said.

Joel walked back to the guy in charge. "Hey, do you have any idea where Carla and Wanda live?"

"Round the corner, 320 East Twenty-Fifth, third floor," said the girl on the couch.

"Thanks."

Joel met Stu at the door. The guys in the corners still had their guns in their laps. As Stu opened it, Joel looked back and said thanks to the guy in charge. He acknowledged with a slow nod.

They left the building and walked down the alley carefully stepping over three of the guys they had fought earlier. Joel and Stu kept an alert eye out for the fourth until they had put some distance between themselves and the alley. "You know we could make a fortune by going gang to gang and offering Martial Arts training," Stu kidded.

"Have fun, Bud. I can think of a lot of other things I'd rather do."

"You're such a wimp!"

"You know what they say, 'Sticks and stones will break your bones, but lead will always kill you.' "

"Aren't you clever?"

Instead of continuing their banter, Joel dialed Jay on his cell. He pushed the speakerphone button just as Jay answered. "It's us, Jay."

"Glad to hear your voice. I tried you a little while ago and got your voicemail. Anything yet?"

"Yeah, things are interesting here, to say the least. We just had a nice little visit with the Judge's, Faxton wasn't there or so they said. We didn't get much information. Supposedly he lives in the building where the gang hangs out. I think we need to call in a favor from LAPD. If they keep watch on the building for a couple of days, they'll know if he's here or not. In the meantime we're gonna check out his girlfriend's apartment."

"Call Ralph Jackson; he's in the Newton Station. Give me a second and I'll find his number. Here it is." He gave Joel the information. "Hey, Stu, you remember Ralph, don't you?"

"Yeah, I'll call him."

"When he left Special Ops he went directly to LAPD and was stationed in their Central Bureau. It has the highest volume of gang-related crime in LA."

"If my memory serves me correctly, they've got the right guy for the job."

"No question about it. I'm sure he'll help you out. After you check out the girl's apartment and talk to Ralph, I want you guys to come back. I'm going to assign you to Reid and Buck. I don't want them walking around without protection and they're very comfortable with you two. Take a red eye to the closest airport you can. Call me when you know where you're going to land. I'll have the chopper pick you up."

"We're gonna need to get Stu stitched up a little before we get on a plane."

"What happened?"

"We had a little skirmish with the Judge's welcome party. No big deal."

"Stu, are you all right?"

"Yeah, just got a small scratch from a knife."

"You sure?"

"Yeah Jay, I'll be fine."

"Well, take care of it. I'll see you both later. Good luck."

"Thanks Jay, see you later," said Joel.

11

In spite of the clear, sunny day, high river winds thrashed at the chopper making for a white knuckle landing. Jay let out a thankful sigh as they touched down, wondering if he was losing his edge. Years ago he would have barely noticed a little turbulence during a chopper landing. Oh well. He opened the cabin door and a windblown Jody climbed aboard.

In a voice loud enough to be heard over the roar of the chopper, Jody yelled, "Leigh and Emma met with the Powers family. It seems Diane went a little over the edge when Bob broke up with her. When Reid told us she was stalking him, he obviously didn't know how serious it was. She had become so uncontrollable they had to institutionalize her. She's been in a behavioral health center in the Princeton area for four months. The girls should be there by now."

"How'd it go with Karen?"

"I think her medication helped us. She offered more information than I expected, without getting pissed off. She didn't react like the hothead that Reid had warned you about. She's still in shock and is an emotional mess, but she explained everything about Bob's affair. She described the scene when she walked in on him and his girlfriend. It was really pretty funny. Even Karen had a good laugh. She gave me detailed descriptions about her conditions for taking Bob back. She also told me about the insurance policy. She held nothing back and was so open with her admissions, I don't believe it was an act. I'm ready to clear her."

"I'm glad. I hate spousal murder incidents. It's so difficult to get an impartial jury."

"Yeah, that's one less problem for us to worry about. How'd you do with Riley?"

"What a character! I'll tell you all about him later, but *he's not* off the hook. I can see him getting excited about setting up a hit. He's got a gun collection that looks more like an arsenal. I noticed a couple of sniper rifles missing. They may have been in the gun cleaner's shop in the basement, but maybe not. I've already requested a search warrant. We'll see."

"Interesting. How did Joel and Stu do with Faxton?"

"Not great. He wasn't at the gang's hangout. Joel and Stu had a little altercation. Now they're headed to Faxton's girlfriend's apartment before they come back on the redeye."

"Anything with the..." Jody was interrupted by the ringing of her cell phone. She answered and listened for a minute. "OK, hold on a minute. I'm with Jay, so let me see who he knows down there." She quickly relayed to Jay that Diane had escaped from the asylum three days ago. The facility had not reported it yet because it was the third escape this year and they figured this one would shut them down. Anyway, besides their own security, nobody's been looking for her. What do you want me to tell Leigh?"

"Give me the phone," he said reaching for her cell. "Hi, Leigh, it's Jay." He listened for a minute as she briefed him. "All right, I'll call Gary Popelka. He's based in Trenton. He'll put an APB out quickly. Before you leave, you need to get Diane's telephone records from the manager. If they give you a problem, call me immediately. I'll have them shut down so quickly, they won't know what hit them. You need to dig up as much information as you can on Diane: who she knows and who visited her lately. Question anyone she spent time with in the facility. I don't have to tell you your job, just dig. Call me as soon as you have anything, OK?" Jay listened, nodded and then hung up.

He scrolled through the numbers in the phone looking for Gary Popelka. "Damn it, I know he's in here. Where the hell is his name?" Just as Jay started to get aggravated, it dawned on him that he had Jody's phone in his hand. He rolled his eyes as he handed it back and pulled his own from his belt clip. Jody was biting her lip to refrain from laughing.

He glanced at her and said, "Go ahead and laugh; it was pretty funny." He found Popelka's number and pressed the dial button. "Captain Popelka, please. Tell him it's Jay Scott." He waited a moment and said, "Yeah, it's me. How are you Gary? It's been a long time." After some quick reminiscing, Jay said, "Hey, I need a favor. I'm working on a case that's branched out into your jurisdiction. Can you put an APB out on a Diane Powers? I'll have one of my investigators call you with details." Popelka responded, then Jay continued, "Thanks, Gary. When this case is closed I owe you dinner. Talk to you soon."

He dialed Leigh again. "Leigh, take this number down. I need you to call Captain Gary Popelka and give him a description of Diane for an APB." As he was giving her the number his phone beeped, "Hold on a second, I have another call." He pressed a button. "Hello"…"Hold on, Joel, let me get rid of another call." He switched back to Leigh. "Leigh, I've got Joel on the other line. Call me later. Keep up the good work."

Jay pressed the speaker button and turned up the volume so Jody could hear. They both huddled close to the phone. "Go ahead, Joel, Jody and I are listening."

"Faxton's not our man."

"That was quick. What did you find out?"

"Well it seems his girlfriend, Wanda, was also dating a guy from a rival gang."

"Uh-Oh!"

"You got that right. We found Faxton and Wanda naked in bed with bullet holes in their heads. They were shot while they were doin' it a couple of days ago."

"*Oooh*! I won't even comment on that. Are you guys on your way back?"

"Yeah, we'll see you in the morning."

"Get some rest. You're gonna need to be alert when you get back."

"No problem. See ya."

"Bye." Jay hung up.

"Yuck." Jody was making a face.

"Nasty image, huh?"

"I'll say."

"What do they say about dying with a smile on your face," Jay said with a snicker.

"*Shut up*!"

Jay laughed then asked the pilot how much longer.

They would be landing at AllSport in about five minutes.

12

The interview team had been busy. They had interviewed well over one hundred people. Most of the discussions were quick and uninformative, but there were three that had proven worthwhile.

Steven Bolson was a soccer player who had also seen the van during his morning run. Steven had been at AllSport for about a year and was being recruited by a bunch of colleges and a few pro teams already. Steven was a little different than most of the other superstars at AllSport. He wasn't cocky and arrogant. He was a good kid and well liked by almost everyone that knew him. The National Youth Soccer Organization had already asked him to be their spokesman. As such, he was going to give talks to kids around the country about what it takes to achieve your potential in the world of soccer. Young players could relate to Steven. He was very intelligent and well spoken, and he enjoyed working with younger kids. Steven had the talent, ability, work ethic, and determination to be the best.

The interview was quick. Before he was asked, Steven said, "I'm pretty sure I've got some helpful information. I saw a Chevy van early this morning near where you guys found Mr. Thomas."

"Excellent, Steven, did you notice anything in particular about the van?" asked the interviewer, Lisa.

"Yeah, it had Pennsylvania plates. I don't know why but I

always look at license plates. I've done it since I was little."

"Well, that is very helpful. Can you remember the number?"

Steven closed his eyes and said, "CCD 439"

"Wow." Lisa said.

Steven smiled. "Photographic memory."

"Unbelievable! Steven, that's great. Give me a second, I'll be right back." Lisa left the room and quickly returned with Chief Wheeler and Jake Mitchell. Jay had put Mitchell in charge of the interview team.

"Hi, I'm Jake Mitchell. Lisa tells me you gave her the license plate number from the van."

"Yeah, my memory just works like that. It made school pretty easy for me."

"Please think hard, Steven, about anything else you saw. Did you see anyone or anything more that you can describe?"

"I really didn't pay much attention. I saw the van and noticed the plate as I ran by but that's pretty much it. I didn't know it was anything important until now."

"Weren't you at the meeting this morning? Why didn't you come forward with this information earlier?"

Steven shrugged, "Sorry. I was at the meeting, but there was no mention about where they found the body. Reid and Buck said they wanted everyone to go about their normal training. That's what I did. I didn't even think about the van until I was told to come here for this interview."

"OK, well you've been a big help. If you think of anything else, please let us know immediately."

Steven nodded and left.

Lisa gave Wheeler the plate number and he called it in.

"How lucky was that," Lisa said. "Well, I guess with over a thousand people on this campus it was only a matter of time till we found *someone* who saw something."

"Kind of makes you wonder, doesn't it?" Mitchell said. "They dumped the body where they knew someone would see it. The arm was lying in plain view. They also took a chance dumping it at five a.m. There would have been a lot less chance of being seen at three o'clock, which goes a little beyond stupid. It's more like they wanted to get caught."

"Interesting thought, Jake," Jay said as he and Jody entered the room.

"Guess you heard that we got the plate number," Mitchell said.

Lisa explained about Steven's photographic memory.

"Any word on it yet, Dave?" he asked Wheeler.

"Just called it in a minute ago. Give it a few."

"Any other relevant information?" Jay asked Mitchell.

"Yeah, a couple of interviews were solid. A basketball player who knew Faxton heard he had plans to off Bob."

"Forget about Faxton. It couldn't have been him because he's been dead for days. I'll fill you in on it later. Tell me what else we have."

Dave, Lisa, and Jake all had surprised looks on their faces. Jake said, "Another athlete, Peter Buckar, an alpine skier who said that he is a good friend of Reid's, gave us some interesting stuff about Hector Vasquez, the boxer who fought with Faxton. Buckar likes to work out in the boxer's gym on the heavy bag. He overheard Vasquez on the phone recently talking to someone about Faxton and Bob. He said there was lots of talk about drugs and weapons and the word kill was used a few times. He remembers thinking that the call sounded as if there was someone from a drug cartel on the other end. It was the last time Buckar worked out in that gym. He figured he took enough risks downhill racing. He has stayed clear of Vasquez ever since."

"Sounds like a smart guy," Jay said.

"That's questionable," Mitchell said. "Did you ever watch a downhill skier? Brains are not a requirement, only balls of steel."

"True enough," Jay said, chuckling. Changing to a more serious tone, he said, "Let's get Vasquez in here. Get a few of his friends also. I really hope this wasn't a cartel hit. Gangs we can handle easily because they're just a bunch of punks. Cartels are another story."

Mitchell called Alan Fox and asked him to find Vasquez and send him over. While he was speaking to Al, Dave's radio beeped. After a quick conversation on his radio, Dave turned to Jay and said, "The van was reported stolen a few days ago. Belonged to a guy who owns a hunting lodge in Equinunk, Pennsylvania, which is about an hour from here. It's a dark blue 2000 Chevy Express. We already added the extra information for the APB. If you want, I'll call Bill Jankowski, the Captain of the Equinunk PD. He'll send somebody to check it out."

"Good, do that, Dave," Jay said. He turned to Jake. "What else do you have?"

"We've done about a hundred interviews. We still have another seven hundred or so. It's going to take another few days, as expected. I'll tell you, though, everyone who knew Faxton figured him for the hit. He didn't have a lot of friends here."

"I thought Faxton might be our man also, but that's all irrelevant now. He was shot a couple of days ago by a rival gang member. Faxton was in bed with his girlfriend and her other boyfriend wasn't too happy about it. Shot 'em both in the head while they were going at it."

"Well, if you gotta go, might as well go out with a smile," Jake said.

"I can't believe you guys," Jody interrupted. "Jay made the same joke. You guys are so warped," she said shaking her head.

The two men glanced at each other, both grinning, then Jay

continued. "All right, let's review what we've accomplished so far." He grabbed a legal pad and handed it to Jody. "Do me a favor, if *you* write this we'll all be able to read it. *I* can barely read my own chicken scratch. I want to list all our original suspects, then discuss what we know about each. I want any incriminating evidence as well as any alibis. First, we've got Karen Thomas. Jody, you cleared her because she readily gave up all the information we thought she would hide if she were guilty. You also said she seemed truly upset, more so than if she was putting on an act."

"That about sums it up," Jody replied.

"OK, I'll agree, we can clear her. Next we have Faxton, but since dead men can't kill…Hey, wasn't there a movie with that name?" he said with one of those "I know this is a bad joke" grins on his face.

Jody rolled her eyes and replied, "How about 'White men can't jump'?"

"Oh yeah, that's it," he said with a chuckle. "Anyway, Faxton's cleared. You can write down Edwin Riley next. He's definitely *not* cleared. I've already requested a warrant to search his house and his phone records. He's got a gun collection unlike any I've ever seen, and I noticed a couple of missing rifles from his wall. Riley is as eccentric as they come and he's loaded. I wouldn't be surprised at all if he hired an assassin." He glanced at his Blackberry. "Next we have Diane Powers, who's also a strong possibility. Leigh and Emma are speaking with people down at a mental rehab facility in Jersey. Turns out Powers went a little nuts after Bob dumped her. She stalked him for months. She escaped from the rehab facility a few days ago. I've got Leigh working with a cop I know down there. We need to beef up the search for her up here. OK, Dave?"

"I'm on it," Dave responded.

"OK, while I spit out a few theories I want each of you to think of possibilities, then each take a turn throwing out your ideas so we can discuss them. Jody, I want you to continue taking notes."

"Would you like fries with that order?" she asked sarcastically.

After a quiet chuckle from the group, Jay continued, "Jake, you said you've interviewed about one hundred people so far. I know you started with the Accounting department. Were you able to get them all?"

"No, there are three people out, including Joe Spinelli. I think you already know he's on vacation climbing Everest. He's due back in a week and a half. I think Reid and Buck have tried to get in touch with him, but it's not an easy task. A Sherpa is on his way to his base camp with the message."

As Mitchell was finishing his explanation, Reid and Buck walked in. They stood at the door while he finished, then walked over and took seats. Buck confirmed the information and added that from now on, if anyone took a similar type of vacation, they would take a satellite phone with them.

"Hey, Reid," Jay said. "We had a skier in here who claims he's a friend of yours. Do you know who I'm talking about?"

"Peter? Why was he here?"

"He had information about a phone call he overheard that might be connected to the case. Do you know him well?"

"Yeah, he's like family. He's really close with my sister. I'm pretty sure they'll eventually get married."

Jay nodded, then continued, "OK, Jake, you said three people from accounting were out, so who are the other two?"

Jake looked at his notes and answered, "Brendan Scanlon and Wendy Ross. Both are auditors. They're in New York at Buck's office auditing ICSF's books."

"When are they due back?"

"They are only supposed to be there for another few days."

"All right, let's make sure they're interviewed as soon as they get back."

Jake nodded.

"Who's got some ideas for me?" Jay asked.

"I do," Jake said. "There were some situations that came up in a few of the interviews with accounting. We heard about two pretty harsh arguments that Bob had fairly recently. One was with the CPA's who used to audit AllSport's books before Bob was hired. It turns out that Bob was never thrilled with them." Jake looked at Buck. "I was told they were your auditors for your own business, right? Then you gave them the ICSF and AllSport accounts as they developed."

"Yup, they seemed like regular guys to me, from one of the big-four accounting firms. Fact is, I never paid much attention to them. They always worked directly with my accounting people. I didn't even know Bob had a problem with them until he recently brought it up. He came to me ready to plead out his case with a long story. He really hated working with them for some reason. I remember he started with an apology because he thought that I had a personal reason for using them, like a friend in their firm or something. He was both shocked and thrilled when I told him I couldn't care less, and he was totally relieved when I said it. He said that he really couldn't stand them but for the last two years he was reluctant to approach me on the subject, thinking I would get pissed off." Buck raised his brow a little and said, "Come to think about it, he seemed pretty excited as he left my office. I remember his last words as he walked out were, 'this is gonna be fun.' He said it in a menacing tone while wringing his hands. I thought it was a little strange at the time."

"Well it got even stranger after that, Buck," Jake said. "It turns out he had the two auditors come up here from New York so that he could fire them in person. He usually sent one of the choppers for them, but this time he told them he didn't have one available. He met with them as soon as they arrived and within minutes things got very loud in his office, so loud almost every word could be heard by those of his people who were nearby. The accountants were furious that he had made them drive two hours just to fire them. The yelling back and forth lasted about five minutes, and it grew in volume as well as vulgarity until the accountants came barging out of his office, blasted through the department, and out the door. They actually shoved one of the doors so hard it cracked and the knob made a hole in the wall."

"Pretty impressive for a couple of CPA's; maybe I should hire them," Jay kidded.

"I wonder why Bob never mentioned it to me," Reid said. "I knew he let them go, but I never heard about the argument."

"There's more," Jake added. "Two of Bob's people said that when he came out of his office a minute later, he had a gleam in his eye like they had never seen before. He said, 'I've been waiting to do that for two fucking years. Oh, that felt good. I hated those self-righteous bastards.' Bob never cursed in front of his employees. In fact, he forbid cursing in the office at all. They all knew he was very strict about it too. They all just listened to him in shock."

"I'm not so surprised," Reid said. "He was a hothead at times. Who's not? If they were on his nerves for that long, his reaction is kind of understandable. But that's only my opinion, and we all know I've blown my cool at times."

Buck and Jay laughed. "Glad *you* said it!" Buck said.

Reid stared at them with smug look and said, "OK, guys, enough." He turned to Jake. "Is that it?"

"No, it didn't end there. There were calls for the next few days from some of the senior partners in the firm. Some of the calls ended in arguments. Bob's secretary actually had to get his phone replaced after he slammed it down and broke it hanging up on one of them. She told us that Bob seemed to enjoy each argument and would grab the phone quickly each time another partner called."

"Did he hire another accounting firm?" Jay asked.

"Of course," Buck said. "With the amount of money we have flowing in and out we need regular auditing. They check our books weekly, sometimes daily, depending on how much cash we've taken in or paid out at any given time. He had another firm on board and working before he let the first one go. Some of the senior partners called me after he fired them. I spoke with a few of them and explained that it was Bob's decision. The calls kept coming but I stopped taking them. As I said, I had no real loyalty to them so it really didn't matter to me, as long as we had a reputable firm watching over us."

"All right, I'm going to need a list of everyone from the firm who worked on the ICSF and AllSport accounts. We'll start with the two guys that came up and fought with Bob. Then we'll also have to speak with the senior partners." Jay looked at Buck and asked, "Is there anyone there that you had a decent relationship with?"

"Yeah sure, I've known Stan Rosen for years. He's the senior partner who originally signed me on as his account. We have lunch together occasionally."

"I'd like you to call him to make sure we get cooperation. I'm sure the entire firm will have an attitude with us."

"I'll call him as soon as we're done here," Buck said.

"Good." Jay turned to Jody. "Let me take a look at the list." He scanned the page and a grin slowly spread across his face as he read.

Everyone noticed his odd reaction. Jody asked, "What's with the grin?"

"It's amazing. I know I've said this before, but usually when we brainstorm, we come up with two, three, maybe four suspects. The only suspect list that I ever saw grow faster than this one was Reid's. Should make for another easy case," Jay pronounced.

Everyone's eyes shifted quickly to Reid. He just shrugged and said, "What can I say?"

"Nothing, I really didn't mean anything by it. It just struck me as funny. Let's move on. Jake, you can get back to your interviews. Joel and Stu are on their way back from L.A. Jody, we are going to have to call in a few more teams to check out some of these leads. But I need to clear my head for a while, and I'm famished. I only had a protein bar for lunch. I'd like to take a walk around campus first, then grab some dinner. Then we can get back together here and put a game plan in place. Jody, will you start breaking down the list and matching it up with appropriate investigators? If you have the time, you can start calling them, and we can send the choppers to pick them up. I'd like to meet with as many as possible first thing tomorrow. Reid, Buck, can we take a walk before getting something to eat?"

"Hold on a moment," Reid said. "I just thought of another possible suspect. A little less than a year ago, Bob fired the artist who created all our statues and trophies. His work was excellent but he was very slow. He kept missing deadlines and it became embarrassing. As you probably noticed, every venue on campus has a life, size bronze statue depicting the venues' sport. Also every athlete who goes pro or to the Olympics gets a bust made and placed within our Hall of Tribute.

"About a year ago, Luigi, the artist, missed a deadline for the opening of our ice hockey venue. It was the first ceremony we had where we did not get to unveil a statue. I told Bob to fire the guy and find a new artist. I also told him to hold up any payments until the hockey sculpture was delivered. A few weeks later I remember Bob telling me that the guy had left some nasty messages and possibly some threatening ones."

"*Possibly*?" Jay asked.

"He didn't say much about them. You should talk to Maria,

Bob's secretary. She should know more. I doubt there's much to discuss. I'm pretty sure the guy is a drunk. It's too bad, because he's a great artist."

"OK, I'll talk to Maria and we'll check him out." Jay looked around the room. "Anybody have anything else to add?"

All remained quiet.

Buck looked at Reid and Jay. "All right let's get out of here." He turned toward the others and said, "Nancy can order you guys something from Champions."

"Jody, Dave, if you want, we've got plenty of sandwiches and salads in the interview waiting area," Jake said. "We always get more information from well-fed interviewees. I can have someone bring you a plate."

"Sounds good," Jody said. "I think I'll come down with you and help myself."

Dave nodded his agreement.

Jay looked at his watch. "It's almost six. Why don't we meet back here at about ten. My radio will be on if you guys come up with anything."

13

As usual Buck had cigars on hand. He handed out Montecristo's along with his cutter and lighter. Jay led the walk through the middle of campus towards the basketball dome, obviously on his way to the crime scene. He asked, "Is there a game in the dome tonight?"

"You can count on one almost every night," Reid said.

"You mind if we watch for a while? I want to go look at the crime scene for a couple of minutes, and then I'd like to go to the game and take my mind off the case."

"Sure, Jay. Do you want to eat at The Winner's Circle afterwards or should I have Nancy make us a reservation off campus?" Buck asked.

"The Winner's Circle will be fine. We can get a private dining room there, can't we?"

"Of course. I'll call now to reserve it." Buck looked at his watch before pushing a button on his cell phone. "Hi Nancy, do me a favor, and call Tom to reserve the back room for us at seven forty-five please." He nodded and added, "Just the three of us." After listening again, he looked at Jay. "Vasquez is up there waiting for Jake right now. Do you want to go back or do you want Jake to deal with him?"

"Let Jake handle him. If we need him afterwards we'll bring him back up."

He finished talking to Nancy by telling her they'd be back before the meeting at ten. Thanking her for all her extra work, he promised to make it up to her after they found the murderer.

Jay lifted the bright yellow crime-scene tape and they all ducked underneath. Jay walked the area slowly and every so often crouched down to take a close look at something. Buck and Reid just watched him and glanced at each other as they both drew on their cigars and allowed the smoke to slowly billow from their mouths. Standing with his hands in his pockets, Jay looked up at the sky and shook his head slightly with a perplexed look.

"I don't get, I just don't get it." He looked at Reid and Buck and continued, "Why the hell would someone shoot him, and then dump his body here to be found? I mean I've investigated plenty of murders. The only ones who ever want the body found are terrorists or someone who's looking to prove a point or scare someone. I'm pretty sure we can rule out terrorists. It's not like he was a public figure or had anything to do with world policies. If it was someone looking to prove a point, it would only make sense if they took responsibility for the hit. If it's somebody looking to scare someone, then who or why?" He tugged gently at his lip in contemplation.

"*I'm* a little scared," Reid said.

"I understand, Reid, but I just don't get how killing Bob is about you. I don't mean any disrespect. This is enough to shake up anyone who went through what you did. But I've already thought about it a hundred different ways and I can't see how this could be attached to your past dilemma. While killing Bob affects you emotionally, it's not the kind of revenge that a gang member is going to seek. If they wanted revenge against you, chances are *you* would be dead instead of Bob."

"Gee, thanks, now I feel much better."

"Reid, seriously, don't get me wrong, you pay me to protect

you and that's exactly what I have been and will continue to do. In fact, I'm going to assign a team to investigate your old gang buddies in Slam. I'm not leaving anything to chance, believe me."

Reid nodded. "Thanks, that's reassuring."

"Good, can we go watch the game now?"

• • •

The whoosh of pressurized air hit them as they pushed through the revolving doors of the dome. Cheering surged through the concrete portals that led to the basketball courts on the floor. As loud as it was, the decibel level was low in comparison to the usual roar of the spectators. The men walked through a tunnel into the stadium. Games were being played on three of the six courts. The game on the closest court looked the most aggressive. Taking positions courtside, the men watched a fierce game. Elbows were flying after each rebound, and the referees were allowing foul after foul without stopping the game.

"Wow, these guys are good, but it looks more like a street brawl than a basketball game," Jay said.

Just as he finished the comment, they saw a fast break with one player way out in front of everyone else. He caught the ball, took two strides, and vaulted towards the hoop. His arm windmilled and he slammed the ball through the net with cannon-like force. The small crowd went crazy. More impressive than the shot was the player's reaction. No gloating, just a quick arm pump as he took off like a cheetah to the other end of the court.

"Holy smokes! He's unbelievable. What a shot. It's like he was floating. And his speed, my God, I've never seen anyone so fast. He should be playing pro ball."

"That's Billy Chambers and he will be soon. We pulled him off the street about a year ago. He was living on a diet of booze and speed, but obviously he had the talent. Our recruiters convinced him to come here and straighten out. He's been clean for a year and his game has improved to the point that he's ready. Now he'll have a tough decision to make, college or pro. He's a pretty smart kid, and he's being watched by a lot of schools, but becoming an instant millionaire is really enticing."

"I guess so," Jay said.

They watched as Chambers flew down the court in another fast break. He caught the ball and was ahead of the pack once again. He launched into the air, spun and slammed a beautiful reverse slam-dunk.

Reid smiled as Jay's two word expletive was drowned out by the scream of the crowd. He tapped Jay and Buck on their shoulders and motioned for them to follow. They walked to the far side of the court and through a heavy blue curtain wall. The court on this side of the divider was empty. Reid grabbed a basketball from a rack and tossed it to Jay. He reached for two more and threw one to Buck. The three of them started dribbling onto the court. As they began to shoot baskets, it quickly became evident that Buck had game.

After his sixth swish in a row, Jay looked over at him with a look of astonishment.

"What you starin' at, man?" Buck asked in an attempt at street slang. "Everyone's gotta be good at something. Reid's got golf, and you've got martial arts and guns. This happens to be my game." He continued to shoot as he spoke, missing very few shots. "I actually had hopes for a pro career after playing at Syracuse."

"I'm impressed. A little shocked too, but very impressed," Jay said.

"Why shocked?"

Jay bit his lip and shrugged.

"Come on, say it."

"Fine, I'll say it. I'm shocked because you're a short, white man. But I'm impressed for the same reason. In fact, I've never thought of you as short. Your attitude and demeanor are quite large, actually, huge. It's kind of funny, I thought I knew you. I guess there are always things to learn about your friends."

"I'll bet there's a lot I don't know about *you*, Jay."

Jay grinned and nodded. "That would be a smart bet." He shot a basket and said, "So tell me a little about your basketball career at SU."

"When I played, the Carrier Dome wasn't built yet. We played at Manley Field House. It was one the best basketball venues I can remember. We had a great team. Do you remember the names Roosevelt Bouie or Louis Orr? They were known as the Louie and Bouie show. They were awesome together. There was also Danny Shayes and Tony "Red" Bruin. I could go on and on. I played through my junior year before it dawned on me that I probably wasn't pro material. My speed and agility compensated for my height. I was good enough for college ball but the pros are a different story. Anyway, I enjoyed the courses I was taking at the business school and an opportunity kind of dropped in my lap. One of the guys being recruited by New York asked me to help him negotiate for a better contract. One thing led to another, and during my senior year I started my agency. Actually, it was like a jump start because I had already negotiated deals for three basketball players and two guys from the football team. After I helped them get good contracts, calls started coming in from other college seniors from various schools. By the time I graduated with my business degree, I already had about twenty clients. I opened an office in Manhattan and the rest is history."

"Very cool story," Jay said.

"This campus is full of good stories," Reid said. "Somebody should write a book about them; it'd probably be a best seller. Seriously, think about it. We've got sports, drugs, death threats, and now, murder. We should hire someone to write about it all. What do you think, Buck?"

"I'm not too sure. I don't think I want to portray AllSport in that light. I think we'd be better off if this is all kept as quiet as possible."

Reid nodded. "Yeah, you're right. Forget about it."

"Anyone ready to eat?" Jay asked.

"I am. Let's go," Reid said.

14

After dinner the three men met Jody, Jake, and Dave Wheeler back up in the boardroom.

"Anybody mind if I light a cigar?" Reid asked.

No objections were heard so Reid walked to a side table and opened a humidor. "Anyone want one?"

All the men accepted and turned to look at Jody. "Oh, what the hell, I'll take one too," she said.

"All right!" Reid said.

"I'll probably regret it later," she said as she picked up a cutter and studied it. "This looks dangerous. Can't I just bite the end off like they do in the movies?"

Jay laughed.

"What are you laughing at?" she asked.

"You! You're proficient with just about every weapon made and you're telling us that a cigar cutter looks dangerous. It just tickled me."

"Yeah, well, precision weapons are one thing, but that thing looks like a finger guillotine. I like my fingers just as they are."

Everyone smiled as Jody bit the end off her cigar.

Soon they all had a glowing red ash at the end of their cigar and smoke was quickly filling the room. The smoke eater in the ceiling was once again put to the test.

"All right, folks," Jay began. "I'd like to keep this meeting short so we can all get to bed. Tomorrow is going to be another long day and I want everyone well rested. Jake, can you give me an update on your interview with Vasquez?"

"First thing I can tell you is the guy is tough to read. He seems fairly smart and kind of smooth. He discussed his fight with Faxton. He said Faxton got pissed at him because he was taking too much time on *his* favorite weight bench."

"There must be twenty weight benches in every gym on campus," Reid said. "Why would he fight over one?"

"That's what Vasquez couldn't figure out. He said Faxton claimed it was his regular bench, and he was able to lift more weights and do more reps when he used it. Vasquez told him to use another bench or just wait. Then Faxton started cursing him out. Vasquez says he got a little nervous and stood up facing Faxton. Faxton shoved him and fists started flying. Vasquez said that the next thing he knew Faxton was swinging a knife. Right after Faxton stabbed Vasquez, Bob ran over with a bar from a weight bench and hit Faxton with it. Bob controlled the situation until security arrived and took both guys to a holding pen in their office. I didn't know you had holding pens on campus."

"If you haven't noticed, most of our clientele here are not exactly Ivy League material," Buck said. "They come from the streets of some of the toughest neighborhoods in the country. Fights are fairly common around here. We are pretty strict with our 'no weapons on campus' policy, but every once in a while something gets in."

Jake nodded. "Interesting. OK, let me finish about Vasquez. He was boiling over with hatred for Faxton, and he felt Bob had saved his life. He figured that if Bob hadn't interfered, Faxton probably would have killed him. He actually seemed upset about Bob's death."

"Or he's using it as a good cover," Jay said. "How did he react when you asked about the phone call that the skier overheard?"

"He said the only call he remembered was to his cousin, a doctor in Columbia. He had to think hard, trying to recall what it was about. He said they talked about a malpractice suit that his cousin is involved in. Somehow a prescription he wrote got confused by the pharmacy and the drug killed the patient. He said the guy's wife came to his office with a gun. She threatened him but couldn't pull the trigger. He said the conversation was in English with a little Spanish mixed in."

"Either he's telling the truth or he's really smooth. Buckar told us he heard talk of drugs and weapons. He heard the word "kill" and thought the conversation sounded like it was to a drug cartel. I'll bet that hearing one side of a phone call with talk of drugs and weapons in a mix of English and Spanish would make just about anyone who doesn't understand the language think that way. My guess is Vasquez probably would have killed *Faxton,* given the opportunity, but I highly doubt he had anything to do with *Bob's* death." Jay rubbed his chin. "I still want to check him out further, but I doubt he's our man. Jody, let's get someone to follow up with his cousin, the doctor."

"I'm already on it. Mench and Greeny are on their way here for tomorrow morning's meeting. Then they're flying to Bogotá immediately afterwards."

"Great, speaking of that meeting, have Joel and Stu checked in?"

"Yeah," Jake answered. "Nancy told us they called before they flew out from LAX, and they should be landing at LaGuardia around two a.m. A chopper will be waiting for them."

Jay nodded and asked, "What else do you have?"

"The search warrant for Riley's place is signed. We should have it in the morning. Judy and Jared are on their way. They'll head out to that hunting lodge in Pennsylvania after the meeting. We have an APB out for Diane in both New Jersey and New York. I've got Lance and Beebs coming up, and after the meeting they're heading down to Manhattan to spend some time with the accounting firm. Chuck Robertson is going to talk to the artist." She looked at her notes. "That's about it so far."

"Let's call it a day." Jay looked at his watch. "It's just after eleven and I want you all to get some rest. Tomorrow's going to be another long day. Let's start here at ten so that everyone traveling can come in fresh and ready. Jody, will you join me for breakfast at eight-thirty at Reid and Buck's house? I want to discuss the day's plan with you before the meeting."

"Of course."

"Jake, can you meet me here at nine-thirty? I think we need to get you a few more people so we can step up the interviewing pace. I don't want to miss any relevant information because we didn't have the manpower to interview everyone quickly enough."

"My interviews start at eight anyway, so just let me know when you get here and I'll come in," Jake said.

Jay turned and looked at Dave Wheeler, "You've been very quiet. Anything new on your end?"

Dave shrugged. "Nothing worth speaking about or you would have already heard from me. Things on campus have been fairly quiet all day. The search for the car continues as it does for Diane Powers. Hopefully, I'll have more for you in the morning."

"Do you have any people available who could help Jake with the interviews?" Jay asked.

Dave thought for a moment. "I don't have a big force, but I know of two troopers who are off on disability. They were in a car accident about a month ago. One is in a wheelchair with two broken legs, and the other is on crutches. They're good, they're smart, and they're both very bored. I'm sure they'll jump at the chance to work with you."

"Probably just not very high," Jay joked.

Dave gave a questioning look then grinned. "Oh, bad choice of words. I had no idea I even said it. Anyway, I'll clear it with their captain and see if I can get them in here tomorrow."

"Good. All right, see you all in the morning."

• • •

Jay's cell phone rang at six a.m. He grabbed it off the night table. "Jay Scott," he mumbled.

"Sorry to wake you, Jay, but we found Bob's car. It's parked at the airport," Dave said.

"The *airport?*"

"I've got eight people here now. We're combing the area. I'll be at the meeting and give you an update then. Tell Jake to expect the two troopers around eight o'clock. They were both pretty psyched when I asked them to help. Coincidently, they both have military backgrounds and are experienced interrogators."

"That'll help. They should fit right in with my team. Good job, Dave. See you in a little while."

Jay hung up and walked to the window; he reached and gave the shade a quick tug. As it went up, what he saw gave him an instant chill. Three men and a woman in dark warm up suits were running on a trail that led into the woods. Jay rubbed his eyes and stared in disbelief. No, his eyes were not playing games with him. The runners had rifles slung over their shoulders with the barrels pointed up in the air.

"What the hell?" he yelled as he grabbed his gun and darted from the room, through the house, and out the back door. He started chasing them and then stopped abruptly, realizing his chances of catching them was slim with bare feet. The fact that he was wearing nothing but boxers didn't faze him. He turned and sprinted back to the house. He had to put someone in pursuit immediately. If he didn't rush, they might kill someone else if they hadn't already. He couldn't let them get away. As he ran into the house, Reid and Buck were both in the kitchen.

"What's wrong? What's going on?" Reid asked.

"Get Alan Fox on the phone, now!" he yelled.

Buck got Fox on his radio and handed it to Jay. "Alan, get a team out here quickly. I just saw four people with rifles running into the woods behind the house. I'm going after them now so make sure your guys know I'm in the woods too. Send one group into the woods from here, and others from wherever you think they may exit the woods. Move on this, Alan, and get as many people as you can combing these woods as quickly as possible."

"Roger that. Out."

Jay quickly put the radio down and turned toward his room. Reid said, "Jay, stop for a second."

He stopped and turned to Reid, "Why?"

"What were the runners wearing?"

"Who gives a damn what they were wearing," Jay yelled, annoyed at Reid for stopping him.

"Were they wearing AllSport warm-up suits? Dark red tops with white stars down the sleeves and dark blue pants with white stripes down the legs."

Jay thought for a moment. "Yes, that's exactly what they were wearing."

"Were they carrying their rifles on their backs, slung tight with the barrel pointed in the air?"

Jay now gave a curious look. "Yes, they were. How did you know?"

"Jay, they're Olympic Biathlon athletes. They train year round on our cross-country trails."

"Oh shit," mumbled Jay rolling his eyes. He grabbed the radio again, pushed the button and said, "Alan, it's Jay. Tell your people to stand down. It was a false alarm. Reid just explained that the people I saw are training for the Biathlon. Do me a favor, stop everyone except four of your people. Send them because I want to be absolutely sure."

"No problem."

"Do me a favor. We're meeting in the boardroom at ten, and I'd like you there."

"All right, I'll see you then."

Jay turned and looked at Buck and Reid. "Well, that was embarrassing."

"Jay, at this point, if you hadn't reacted as you did, *that* would be embarrassing," Buck said.

"I'll get over it. Always better to be safe." He looked at the clock. "It's only six-thirty, will you guys take a walk with me? I'd like to get a little exercise before the day gets rolling. It's going to be another long one."

"Let's walk the back nine," Reid said. "We just changed the sand in a couple of the bunkers and I want to check it out."

"Changed the sand?" Jay asked.

"Yeah, I like to work in different grades and consistencies. You never know what type of beach you're going to have to play out of on tour."

"Interesting. I'm always amazed at how much I learn around here. I'm going to put on some clothes. I'll be ready to go in a minute."

"Anyone want a cigar?" Buck asked.

"No, thanks," said Reid.

"Jay?"

"No, I'm gonna pass too."

"Guess this'll be my first cigar-less walk in a long time."

"Go ahead light up, Buck. We don't mind," Reid said.

"Nah, I'm not going to be accused of polluting the air on your precious golf course by myself."

"Bet you can't make it for nine holes without firing one up," Reid said.

"What's the bet?"

Reid thought for a second. "Let's make this interesting. If you make it, I'll write the check for the down payment on the boat. If you light up, then you write the check."

"You got it, man. This is going to be the easiest million I've taken from you yet."

"A million dollar deposit! What the hell are you guys buying, an ocean liner?" Jay asked.

"A 125-foot Trident," Buck said. "It's a beautiful boat. We just gave them a verbal commitment last week."

• • •

Close to the end of their walk, on the sixteenth fairway, Buck pulled out and clipped a cigar. He smiled as he put it in his mouth, knowing that Reid and Jay were watching him in astonishment. He played with the cigar, turning it in his mouth as they walked. He pulled his lighter out of his pocket on the seventeenth green. The desire to light the stogie was getting the better of him. He pushed the button, lighting the flame a couple of times, but letting it go out each time. Finally, as they walked off the eighteenth green, he lit the cigar with a big smile, looked over at Reid, held up his hand, and pushed his index finger down on an imaginary cash register button while saying, "Cha-ching."

Reid smiled at him and winked.

• • •

The boardroom was crowded. After quick hello's between the investigators who knew each other and introductions between the rest, Jay started the meeting.

"I'm sure by now all newcomers have been briefed by Jody. Does anyone here *not* know the situation?"

No hands were raised and all remained quiet.

"Good. Well let me start by having Dave Wheeler, the Chief of Police, explain about finding Bob's car."

Dave stood. "Well, Jay, as you know we found Bob's BMW at the Greater Binghamton Airport. The car was brought in and is being searched and dusted as we speak. It had been parked in the long-term lot, and we searched the immediate and surrounding areas. Not a trace of blood or any other evidence of the kill could be found. There were no buildings above one story within sniper range. We checked the paths from the car to each of two airline departure entrances. Again nothing. Although I can't imagine why, it looks as though the hit took place elsewhere, and then the car was driven to the airport. We're searching the entire route from Bob's house to the campus for a second time.

I have a few detectives searching around the deli where he usually stopped for coffee. Rocky, the owner of the deli, confirmed that Bob did not come in that morning. One of the store's employees recalled seeing a van double-parked on the side street, next to the deli, as he came to work that day. The rear doors of the van were open and there was at least one guy unloading it, or so he thought. He figured it was just a delivery for the deli. When we asked if the guy could have been putting something in the van instead, he said he really didn't think much about it since deliveries are always coming in. He did say it was a possibility, though. We're scouring the area right now, as well as checking the surrounding rooftops and buildings, anywhere the shot could have been taken. I'll let you know the minute we find anything. Our search for Diane Powers has yielded nothing yet."

"Thanks," Jay said. He turned towards Alan Fox. "For those of you who don't know Alan Fox, he's Director of Security here at AllSport. Alan, can you give us a quick campus update?"

Alan stood. "Last night we caught another fame-seeking athlete getting interviewed by a reporter. One of my guys, Mario Barrata, was escorting the reporter through campus as per your instructions. Mario made the mistake of allowing the reporter to use the bathroom in the basketball dome by himself. When the reporter took a little too long, Mario went in and, sure enough, the reporter was interviewing Matt Mango, one of our star quarterbacks. I would hate to throw Matt out of here because he's a good guy and he'll probably go pro really soon. I don't know what gets into their heads; every athlete knows they're not supposed to give interviews, yet they are ready to put their career on the line as soon as they get a chance to be in the news. I'll let you guys decide on Matt."

"What do you mean, let us decide?" Reid said. "We made the rule for a reason and we'll stick to it. Send him home. You know what'll happen if we allow him to stay; tomorrow we'll have more of the same and it will keep on getting worse. No way. He's out. That's final." Reid's tone was venomous.

Brows raised and silenced whistles passed through puckered lips.

"OK then...Let's move on. I want to bring you all up to date on the suspect list." Jay read through the list and gave everyone their specific jobs. Those traveling by chopper left immediately. On Chopper I, Lance and Beebs were on their way to investigate the employees of the CPA firm in Manhattan. Also on board were Chuck Robertson, Bill, and Keith who would all be dropped off at Westchester Airport. Robertson was heading to the artist's home-based studio, while Bill and Keith were going to search Edwin Riley's house. Chopper II was carrying Mench and Greeny to Newark Airport to catch a flight to Bogotá, Columbia. Also onboard were Leigh and Emma. They were headed to New Jersey to assist in the search for Diane Powers.

Judy and Jared took one of the campus Hummers to check out Adam, the hunting lodge owner in Pennsylvania.

Joel and Stu were back on duty as Reid and Buck's bodyguards. "Here we go again, huh guys?" Reid said.

"Sorry, dude, looks like you're stuck with us one more time," Joel said. "Hope you're not *too* upset about it."

"Nah, if I have to have protection it might as well be you guys."

"Now ain't that a vote of confidence," Stu said.

"Oh, don't start; you know what I meant," said Reid.

"I guess," Joel said.

Reid rolled his eyes and walked away.

15

A police cruiser was waiting at Westchester Airport for Bill and Keith as they landed. Jay had arranged for two officers to help search Riley's house. As Bill and Keith were getting in the car, Chuck Robertson, always the clown, tried to get in next to them. Bill said, "Sorry, Chuck, you'll have to take a cab or rent a car."

"Come on, give me break. Shove over and make room." He sat on the edge of the back seat and started to squeeze in.

"I'm serious, Chuck," Bill said. "Get your fat butt out of here now. We don't have time for your shenanigans."

"Oh, calm down, will you? I was only fooling around. Officers, do me a favor, would you? Leave him at Riley's house when you're done with the search, OK?"

"Yeah, sure. Whatever you say pal," said the cop in the passenger seat. "Just get out of the car already so we can get to work."

"All right, all right. I can take a hint. I know when I'm not wanted. Don't be so subtle next time." He got out of the car with a smirk on his face, and closed the door. "See you guys back at All-Sport."

"Good luck with the artist," Bill said.

"Thanks, good luck on your search. See you later."

"Later, man." Bill stuck his fist out the window and Chuck tapped it with his.

• • •

The Crown Vic's wheels spun as the officer driving hit the gas. "Is that guy always such a clown?" he asked.

"Pretty much," Bill said. "He's usually pretty funny."

"If you say so." Just a few minutes later they pulled up to the gates at Riley's house.

The officer lowered his window and pushed the button on the speaker.

"May I help you?" came a female voice through the speaker.

"Yes, ma'am, I'm Officer Roland. Could you please open the gate?"

"May I ask why you're here, officer?"

"Are you Mrs. Riley?"

"Yes, I am."

"Mrs. Riley we have a warrant to search your home."

"May I see it?"

"Sure, open the gate and I'll bring it to you."

"Just hold it facing the speaker, please," she said in a no-nonsense tone.

Roland squinted, searching for the camera. He found it and rolled his eyes, annoyed that he had missed it.

"That's right, officer, smile for the camera. Now, may I see the warrant?"

Roland, doing his best to control his temper, unfolded the warrant, aggressively snapped it open, and stuck it in front of the camera.

"Back a little, please," came her irritated voice.

He moved it back.

"A little more, officer; I can't quite read it yet."

He pulled it further away. Fury was building inside him. The other three men were doing their best to contain their laughter.

In spite of his efforts, Keith let a loud snort slip out.

"Is something funny, gentlemen?" she asked dryly.

Roland finally could take no more. "Ma'am, stop the games and open the gates now. There are two types of searches we can perform. The first is where you cooperate. The second is where you keep acting as you are. Believe me, you don't want the second."

"Is that a threat?"

"No, ma'am, but if you don't open the gates right now you will be hearing the threat of arrest. Open them *now,* ma'am."

As the gates opened and they drove in, the three others in the car burst out in laughter. Roland had to breathe deeply to calm down. "Keep laughing, you idiots, but when we get to the house you better keep her away from me, otherwise I may just kill her."

"Calm down, John," Roland's partner said. "Take some deep breaths; we have to be level-headed during this search."

"I'm OK."

They all gasped as they pulled up to the mansion. "Holy shit," Keith said. "This place looks more like a castle than a house. It's huge. This is going to take more than one day. Can you guys get more help?"

"I'll call in a request," Roland said. "There should be a patrol car in the area."

He called in and explained the situation to his chief and then turned to the others and said, "My chief will be here soon, along with two other officers. He got curious after hearing about Mrs. Riley's attitude. He thinks it might be more fun to search an eccentric millionaire's mansion than shuffle paper at his desk."

"I'll bet. OK, guys, let's do it," Bill said.

They exited the car and walked up the brick steps to the massive front door. As Roland went to push the intercom button, the door slowly opened. "Please, come in, gentlemen," said a tuxedo-clad butler. "I'm sorry but Mr. Riley is not home at the moment and Mrs. Riley is not feeling well. She said to let you in and offer my services if I can be of help."

"Not feeling well, huh?" Roland said.

"Correct, sir. She seems to have acquired a terrible headache."

"No doubt I had something to do with it."

"Quite possibly, sir."

Bill interjected, "We may need some help finding things around the house. I'd bet you know this house better than anyone, right? I'm sorry, I'm afraid I never caught your name."

"It's William, sir."

"William, huh? Well, William, it's nice to meet you. I'm Bill."

They smiled as they shook hands.

"Can you show us to Mr. Riley's office? I'd like to see all the statements for the home phone and the cell phones."

"They won't be in Mr. Riley's study. They are filed in the bookkeeper's office, which I'll show you if you'll follow me."

Bill looked at the others. "Let's split up. I think two of you should go through Riley's study. We are looking for anything that may relate to Faxton. Also look for anything connected to Riley's time in the joint. Possibly relationships he made in lockup whom he still communicates with. See if you can find a daily planner or any other type of calendar." Bill thought for a second and then continued, "When the others get here we'll map out the rest of the house and break up into more efficient teams." He turned back to William. "Do you think you could draw a diagram of each floor of the house?"

"No need, sir, it's already done. I will make copies of the architectural floor plans we give to anyone who services the house. It saves me a lot of time."

"Keith, why don't you come with me, and let's see what we can find," Bill said.

• • •

Five hours later the group converged in the study. With the help of the two additional officers and their chief, they had searched most of the house. Having found nothing incriminating, they reconvened to search the three remaining areas; the gun collection, shooting range, and garage. They had agreed to save these for last and search them as a team.

William assisted with the elevator. Waiting for it to arrive, they heard a door slam somewhere in the direction of the garage. A loud yell followed, "What the hell is going on here?"

Edwin Riley stormed into the elevator lobby. A couple of the officer's chuckled at the sight of him: Pointy, lizard-skin cowboy boots, ten-gallon Stetson, and a wide belt studded with a row of vertically lined bullets all the way around his massive girth, finishing at a huge gold buckle with ER emblazoned on it.

"What is this, a freakin' raid? I want you all outta here now," he yelled with rage. "The only way you are getting back in my house is with a warrant. Now get out!"

Bill walked right up to him, snapped open the warrant and held it out for Riley's inspection. Riley grabbed the paper from Bill's hand and studied it. "Hmph," he grunted as his face contorted in fury. His free hand turned a little white as he clenched it into a tight fist. His face turned red and his entire body seemed to tremble. "This is a bunch of crap. I've done nothing wrong." As he realized he was powerless to stop the search, he calmed a little and took a deep breath. "Oh, whatever. I have nothing to hide. Go ahead and search until you're content. I need a drink."

He spun around and walked into his study. Bill followed him and watched Ed fill a highball glass with bourbon, sit in his easy chair, and light a cigar.

"Mr. Riley, at this point we have searched everything except your gun and car collections. So far you have nothing to worry about, except a few recent calls you've made to John Umeana."

"Umeana? That punk! I met him in jail. He told me he could get some rare guns. He was full of crap; just another hustler trying to rip me off."

"Well, Ed, if that was all, I probably wouldn't care about him. Turns out, he's connected, though."

"Connected?"

"Yeah, Ed, as in Mafia. And what's even worse is that he's a suspected hit man."

"Hit man?" Ed said wide-eyed. "Oh, great." Ed gulped down the rest of his drink.

"Right, Ed. Your only saving grace at the moment is that he has been behind bars for the last few weeks."

Ed let out a sigh.

"Don't get too comfortable. It's easy to set up a hit from jail, especially for a wiseguy."

"Damn, I swear I only asked him to get me some guns. It had nothing to do with a hit. I had nothing to do with that murder, nothing!"

"We'll see, Ed. In the meantime, please stay put while we finish our search. I may want to speak with you afterwards."

"I'll be right here," Ed said as he poured himself another generous drink.

"Try to stay coherent, Ed."

"Sure." He nodded as he took another long pull on his bourbon.

By the time Bill got back to the elevator, the group had already gone down to the gunroom. William was waiting for him and brought him down. The search of the gun collection was long and tedious. With gloved hands, every gun was checked for signs of recent firing. Johnny, the gun cleaner, came out of the cleaning room and looked around with curious suspicion.

"Who are you?" Keith asked.

"I'm, Johnny, and I work for Mr. Riley. I clean his guns and take care of the range."

"Tell me, Johnny, I see the outlines for some missing guns on the wall. Are they in your cleaning shop?" Bill asked.

"A couple of them are. The two over there are not." He pointed to an area on the wall where the outlines for two rifles surrounded empty hooks.

Bill walked over to take a closer look with Roland. They both looked at the outlines, then looked at each other with raised brows. "Johnny, could you come here?" Bill asked.

As Johnny got close, Bill said, "These outlines look like sniper rifles. What's the make and model of the guns that belong here?"

Without hesitation he said, "Both were .308 caliber Brown Precision Tactical Elite rifles, and both had standard four-shot magazines."

"Impressive, and you say they are not in your cleaning room. Where are they?"

"Couldn't tell you. They've been gone for about two weeks. I mentioned it to Mr. Riley the day I saw that they were missing. He told me not to worry about them."

"Interesting," Roland said.

"Very," Bill agreed.

They finished searching the gun room, the range, and the cleaning shop, before heading back up to the first floor.

Bill, Keith, and Chief Baloy entered the study to find Riley sprawled in his recliner, head back, mouth wide open and snoring loudly.

Bill walked over. "Ed, Ed, wake up." He kicked the bottom of Ed's boot. "Hey, Ed, wake up. We need to talk to you."

Ed barely opened one eye. "Huh, whaddya want?" he slurred.

Bill looked at the empty Jack Daniels bottle on the table next to Ed.

"So much for him. Let's go to the garage and finish the search. We'll deal with him afterwards."

They entered the garage with anticipation. Remarks of awe came from each of them. After searching for about an hour, they got ready to head back to Riley.

Bill took one more look around the huge garage. Something was bothering him.

"What's the matter?" Keith asked.

"I don't get it. I mean I've never seen a garage this big, but it doesn't make sense to me that there are six overhead doors on that wall facing the driveway. Then there is a double overhead door that faces the side of the property." He started walking towards the door with Keith.

They went to opposite sides of the door. Keith found and pushed the button.

The door rose slowly to reveal a separate four-bay garage. In one bay was a large tractor. The second bay held a pickup truck with a plow. In the third bay were various golf course maintenance vehicles. And parked in the fourth bay was a dark blue Chevy van.

Bill and Keith looked at each other with grins. They walked to the van and, with their gloved hands, tried to open the doors. No good; they were all locked. A quick walk around the van revealed splattered mud around the rear wheel wells and fenders.

"New York plates," Bill said. "Well, at least he was smart enough to change those."

"You'd think the idiot would have at least dumped the van somewhere else," Keith said.

"I'm not sure if it's stupidity or arrogance," Bill said. "But things are adding up pretty quickly, aren't they? We've got phone calls to a hit man, missing sniper rifles, and now a van matching the description of the vehicle at the crime scene. I'd say Mr. Riley is about to do some more time. What do you think?"

"I'd say the sentence he'll get for this will make his last stint behind bars seem like a quick vacation."

The others had circled around. "He'll get twenty to life if he gets a day," said Roland's partner.

"There's a good chance he'll get a death sentence. Conspiracy to commit capital murder won't get off easy," Baloy said.

"Can one of you call for a flatbed?" Bill asked. "We need to bring this thing in to get dusted and examined. The tread will also need to be compared to the imprints we pulled from the scene. I've got to call Jay."

He dialed Jay on his cell and held it to his ear. After explaining the situation and listening to Jay's response, he hung up. Turning to the others, he said, "Jay wants to get some answers before we bring Riley in. We need to see what we find out about the van, and we'll have to ask Riley where the two rifles are and follow up. Jay is going to call me back with anything he can find out about Umeana, our hit man. If he's in jail, Jay will find out where. If he's out and he's mobbed up, Jay has the contacts to find out where he hangs out. Wherever it is, Keith and I are heading there right away. Can one of you take us back to the airport to rent a car?"

"If it's Manhattan or one of the boroughs, I'll take you there myself," said Baloy. "Riley's in my jurisdiction, and if nailing him means we have to find this guy first, I want to be there."

"Thanks, chief, I hope you don't mind if I make two requests. First, would you mind changing into plain clothes? Second, can we drive something unmarked, such as your own private car if possible? Something about showing up at a Mafia hangout with a cop doesn't thrill me."

"No problem, I agree."

"Can you also post one or two men out on the street here, in case our friend gets the jitters when he sobers up? I don't want to take any chances on him running."

"Done. I'll put round-the-clock surveillance on him." He turned to Roland. "John, you and Jimmy can start. When do you go off duty?"

Roland looked at his watch. "About an hour ago, but if it's OK with Jimmy, I'd like do the first shift. I want to be here for the bust if you guys get the evidence you need."

They looked at Jimmy, "Hey, I'm in. Let me just call my wife and let her know. I wouldn't miss this for anything."

"I'll send relief at twelve," Baloy said. "I don't want you two burning out. You've already put in a long day."

Bill's phone rang. He checked the caller ID and answered it. "Yeah, Jay, go ahead." He listened. "Mario's, yeah I know it. It's on the Upper East Side. We'll call you after we talk to him." He hung up and looked at the others.

"This should be fun. Ever been to Mario's? It's an interesting place with lots of celebrities and lots of mob. No reservations, though. You need to know someone who owns a table. Umeana's crew has a table there tonight. He should be there all night. Let's see how our friend inside is feeling before we go."

"Now how the hell did Scott get that information?" Baloy asked. "If I didn't know his reputation, I would have guessed he was connected too."

"Jay has more sources than anyone," Bill said, "especially in New York."

They walked inside, and after a quick check on Riley, they thanked William for his help and left.

"Tell Mrs. Riley that I hope she's feeling better," Roland said sarcastically.

"Yes, sir," said William with a smile and a wink.

16

The drive to Pennsylvania had turned up nothing. Adam, the owner of the hunting lodge, laughed when he heard that Judy and Jared were there to check out his story.

"Look, I'm flattered that you're even taking the time to check me out. But not only didn't I have anything to do with any murder, I've never even heard of Bob Thomas. I *wish* my life was that exciting. I manage this lodge and I take groups hunting and fishing. That's it."

"What can you tell us about the van that was stolen?" Jared asked.

"It was a dark blue Chevy Express work van: low mileage, no dents, pretty clean. I really don't use it very often; I use my pickup most of the time. I was gone the day it was stolen, riding my horses with my kids. I didn't even notice it was gone when we got back. My son asked where it was and I told him that I had no idea. I called Jankowski immediately. One of his guys already took a report, but I guess you probably know that, right?"

Judy nodded and asked, "Are the keys missing?"

"Yes."

"Where do you keep them and who has access?"

"On a shelf just inside the door, and as far as access is concerned, I guess anybody who wants it. We don't lock doors around here. We're pretty deep in the woods and there's not a lot of trouble in the area. Every once in while there's a fight at one of the campgrounds on the river. But I don't remember the last time something was stolen."

"One last question, and then we'll leave you alone," Jared said.

"Go ahead, fire away."

"What do you think about AllSport?"

Adam shrugged. "Never really thought much about it. I play a little golf, but *my* sports are hunting and fishing. They don't train on either at AllSport, at least as far as I know. The campus has brought some jobs to the area. That's always a good thing. But besides that it really doesn't affect my life at all."

"Well, we appreciate your time," Judy said. "We'll be in touch if we need anything further."

"You know where to find me."

As they left, Jared reported into Jay who told them to come back to campus and help with the interviews.

• • •

Lance and Beebs hadn't expected things to go easily at the CPA firm, but they hadn't figured on a battle at every turn either. The entire firm was giving them a hard time. The partners were pissed off that they were even suspected of any possible connection to Bob's death. As the day went on, Lance and Beeb's view changed as they spoke with each partner. With some, they felt there was animosity for the loss of the accounts. AllSport and the ICSF were the firm's biggest and most profitable accounts and losing them took money directly out of each partner's pocket. Others felt that, even being suspected of such a heinous crime, was tantamount to a public false accusation. They knew word was already out within the accounting industry that they had lost the account. They also knew that some of their existing clients had originally come to them solely because they were AllSport's accountants, and the same clients would probably leave them now. The fallout would get even worse when the press got hold of the information.

Each attempt at an interview brought on a different reaction. Some partners wouldn't let them into their offices. Some simply refused to answer any questions. Some ranted and raved from the minute they entered. One threw a mug at them, which shattered against the wall, spraying coffee all over the white wall and carpet. The guys actually looked at each other in surprise and laughed out loud at that one.

They had some success with Stan Rosen, the senior partner, who was smart enough to realize that the best way to handle the situation was to give them the answers they wanted and end the painful charade as quickly as possible. The two accountants who had taken the brunt of Bob's ill feelings were pissed off, but at least willing to speak. They knew they had to be at the top of the list of suspects within the firm. They admitted they were upset the day that Bob fired them, but who wouldn't be. Bob had requested that they drive all the way from Manhattan to AllSport just so he could fire them and send them back home.

Lance and Beebs agreed it was a pretty rotten way for Bob to have handled it, but it certainly wasn't reason to kill him.

The accountants gave Lance and Beebs enough information to prove their innocence. They both had strong alibis.

Lance called Jay and reported the entire situation. Jay cleared the two accountants, but added the names of the partners who had acted inappropriately. Jay realized that he and Buck would probably have to deal with the partners themselves. He told Lance and Beebs to clear out and to head over to Mario's restaurant to assist Bill and Keith if it became necessary.

17

Dressed in plain clothes, Chief Baloy was guarding the entrance to Mario's. He was not allowing anyone to enter the restaurant. Two couples were at the door arguing with him when Lance and Beebs arrived. They assumed Baloy was a wiseguy. Hearing a louder argument taking place inside, they decided to go in. Baloy blocked their way saying, "Sorry, gentlemen, we are full at the moment. You'll have to wait till some of the guests leave."

The door to the restaurant was open just enough to hear the argument inside getting louder. The brick front of the building was windowless, providing an additional level of protection to those inside, but also preventing the guys from being able to evaluate the situation within. Lance said, "We just need to go in and give a message to a friend. We'll come right out after that and wait."

"I'm afraid I can't allow that."

"And I'm afraid I'm running out of patience," Lance said as he reached for the door.

Baloy grabbed Lance's wrist in an attempt to twist his arm and force him up against the wall. Baloy hadn't figured on what came next. Lance twisted his arm out of Baloy's grip and with a quick spin turned the situation around so he was holding Baloy up against the wall.

Shocked, Baloy managed to say, "You've got to be one of Jay Scott's men."

"Who are you?" Lance asked.

"I'm Chief Baloy. I'm here with Bill and Keith, and they're inside already. I was blocking the door to give them time. Let's go in. It sounds like they may need help."

Lance released Baloy and the three of them went in. Once inside the dining room, they immediately saw the severity of the situation. Bill and Keith were seated at a table in the middle of the room. Four rather large men were standing with their automatics pointed at them. Another two goons held guns with their muzzles at each of the men's temples. Bill and Keith's hands were palm down on the table. Bill was in the middle of explaining that they were looking for Umeana. Half the patrons in the dining room were under their tables. The other half were sitting at their tables just watching. A few actually continued eating their meals and watched as if it was the evening's entertainment. *Only in New York*.

Lance motioned with his eyes to Beebs and Baloy that they should all go over to help. Slowly, they walked around the tables with their hands raised in the air. All eyes had shifted towards them. Lance said in a very calm voice, "Gentlemen, no one needs to get hurt here. We only came to ask John Umeana a few questions. If he's here, let us speak with him and we'll be on our way. If he's not, we will leave without any problems."

"Are you cops?" asked an older gray-haired man with a heavy Italian accent.

"No. We're private investigators. We're trying to nail a guy for a murder and we think Umeana can help us."

"Tell me how."

"The guy we like for the murder did time with Umeana. Umeana mentioned to him that he could get him guns. If we can find out what kind of guns Umeana supplied him, we should be able to pin him for the murder."

"Who got killed?"

"The Chief Financial Officer for the Inner City Sports Foundation. Maybe you've heard of it; it's the Foundation that Reid Clark...."

"Of course I know about it," the older man interrupted. He held up his hand, showing Lance his ring. "I've been a contributor ever since Reid and Buck started it. I love AllSport. That's one tough golf course they designed there. I play it every year when I go up for the ring holder's weekend. Tell you what, if Umeana can help you nail the bastard, then give me a way to contact you. I'll set up a meeting tomorrow. For now, why don't you all join me? The food here is unbelievable; you're gonna love it. By the way, I'm Sal." He gave the men at his table a nod, motioning for them to get up and give their seats to Lance and the others.

The guns had all disappeared. Some of his men got up immediately. Some of them just looked at him in astonishment. He stared them down with powerful eyes. Obviously they knew not to argue. They got up from their seats and walked away, mumbling.

Lance, Beebs, Bill, Keith, and Baloy all sat a little reluctantly at his table.

"I'm gonna order for the table if that's all right with you." He nodded his head in the direction of the nearest waiter who was at his side in a flash. "Franco, we're gonna start with some Antipasti. Bring one hot and one cold. Then bring us some Linguine Vongole, and have Dino throw in some shrimps and calamari too."

"Red or white sauce?" the waiter asked.

He paused for a moment in thought, then said, "Make it red. Then we'll have the Vitello Mario and some Melanzane Parmigiano." He looked around the table. "Anybody want anything else?"

They all shook their heads.

"One more thing, Franco. Bring some sautéed escarole." After another quick thoughtful pause he added, "That should do it."

The waiter started to leave. "Send Gino over with a few bottles of my Chianti Classico. There should be a full case downstairs."

They all ate until they were stuffed except Baloy who barely touched the food. He was uncomfortable even sitting at the table.

"What's the matter?" Sal asked Baloy. "You want something else? How about some chicken. The Chicken Scarpariello is excellent; it's what I usually order."

"No, thanks. My stomach is acting a little funny tonight, that's all."

"Suit yourself."

Lance picked up a bottle of wine and studied it. Castello Di Ama Vigneto, Bellavista—Chianti Classico.

"You like it?" Sal asked.

"Like it? I love it!"

"Me too. Wine Spectator rated it ninety-five. I visit the vineyard regularly and have a few cases shipped back. Take a bottle with you when you go."

"No, I couldn't."

"You can and you will."

"Well, if you insist. Grazie."

"Prego!"

They finished the meal, but Sal wouldn't let them leave until they had dessert, espresso, and Grappa. They finally left after he reconfirmed that he would call Lance the next day to confirm the meeting with Umeana.

They walked about a block before they all fell apart laughing. Keith said, "Wow, that was exciting; I thought Bill and I were gonna get capped for a minute there."

"Yeah, I thought so too," Bill said. "Good job, Lance, we owe you. You turned that whole thing around. First, with only wanting Umeana for the gun information, then with the whole ICSF and AllSport smokescreen."

"Hey, I just got lucky. Who would have guessed a freakin' mob boss would have an AllSport ring."

"Do any of you even know who he was?" Baloy asked.

None of them had any idea.

"That was Sal DiGiacomo."

Their eyes grew wide. "You mean the head of the DiGiacomo crime family?" Beebs asked.

"You got it. I can't believe I just had dinner with him."

"Don't worry, Chief, if you think about it, you really didn't because you didn't eat anything," Bill said. "In fact, you really look kinda sick. Are you OK to drive home?"

"Yeah, I'll be all right. Any of you need a ride?"

"No, thanks, we're going to get a couple of hotel rooms," Lance said. "I want to be close when DiGiacomo calls for the meeting. I need to call Jay and give him an update." He pushed Jay's number into his cell phone and pressed the speaker for all to hear.

"Hi, Jay, got a minute?"

"Yeah, go ahead."

"Umeana wasn't there but you'll never guess who was. We just had dinner with Sal DiGiacomo."

"Really, let me think. I'll bet you started with antipasto, then pasta with seafood, then either the Veal or Chicken Mario with some vegetable on the side. Then, when you thought you were going to explode, he made you have dessert and after dinner drinks."

They were all silent.

"Hello, anybody there?" Jay kidded, obviously enjoying himself.

"You never cease to amaze me, Jay. I guess it won't surprise you that he is setting up a meeting with us and Umeana. In fact, when he heard who was murdered, he really wanted to help us out."

"Sal is a good man. I may not agree with the way he does business, but he has a big heart. He's helped me with many cases."

"What's he doing with an AllSport ring? You can't tell me Reid and Buck accept his donations, do they?"

"No, they don't. But whenever we have a team traveling to other parts of the country or world for that matter, Sal makes sure they have plenty of security. He has more connections than anyone I know. No pun intended."

"Doesn't it take at least a million dollar donation to get a ring?" Bill asked.

"That's right," Jay answered.

"That's a lot of security," Beebs said.

"All right, all right, let it go, guys. So tell me, what time is this meeting with Umeana?"

"We don't know yet," Lance said. "DiGiacomo is going to call me tomorrow with the details."

"I'd like you to meet with him early. I think I'll call Sal and get things moving. You guys should get some sleep so you're fresh and ready to go when he calls."

"All right, Jay, good night," Lance said.

"Night."

18

Jay walked from his room, bleary-eyed. He was amazed he had slept until eight o'clock. He never slept late during an investigation. His internal alarm usually woke him by six. He was a little annoyed that he had lost the two hours, although he knew he probably needed the extra sleep.

Reid and Buck were in the living room drinking coffee. "Morning," Buck said. "Ready for another fun day?"

"I'm not sure about fun but at least I feel like we're making headway." He went to the kitchen, poured himself a cup of coffee and walked back to the living room. Standing by the massive windows, he stared outside. "Hopefully we'll get a quick confession out of Umeana today. I'm really looking forward to busting Riley, that arrogant son of a bitch. It would be nice to wrap this thing up so we can bury Bob in peace. When is the funeral?"

"I think Karen decided on Saturday so that his staff from here could all be there," Reid said quietly. "He's being cremated. The service is at his church, followed by a gathering at their house. Bob wanted Karen to sprinkle his ashes in the water behind the house."

Jay nodded in acknowledgment.

Reid sighed and shook his head. "I still can't believe he's gone. Anytime I'm sitting around like this, I kind of expect him to walk into the room and make one of his dumb jokes. Pretty silly, huh?"

"Not at all," Jay said. "It's only been a couple of days. It would be odd if you didn't feel that way."

Reid shrugged.

Jay lifted his coffee mug to his lips and drained it. "I'm going to get cleaned up and head over to help with the interviews. You guys can lay low today. I'll give a yell if anything comes up."

"I need to get out on the golf course. I have a tournament coming up, and I haven't even swung a club in the last few days. I hate playing when I'm uptight; it screws up my whole game. I may have to back out of the tournament."

"It would be understandable if you did," Buck said.

"We'll see. I'd like to play, but not if I'm going to be an emotional wreck."

"Can we reserve judgment on the final decision?" Jay asked. "I want to see how this whole thing plays out first. I'm not sure I want you out in the crowds until we're absolutely sure who did this."

"I'm hoping it's Riley and Umeana," Reid said. "I would feel a lot safer if it's not connected to *my* shooting in any way."

"We all would," Jay said.

"Well, if you don't need us, Jay, then I should get some work done. It's been piling up and I don't want to let it get out of hand." Buck looked at Reid. "That is, unless you want company on the golf course."

"Thanks, but I could use some time on my own. Oh, I forgot, I'm not allowed to be on my own, not with Joel and Stu around."

"Where are they anyway?" Jay asked. "I need to speak with them."

"Out on the patio in back," Buck said.

Jay started in that direction.

"Jay, do me a favor. Let Joel know that he and I are going to play eighteen holes."

"Sure, I'll tell him, but why not Stu?"

"Because I've seen Stu hit golf balls before, and he sucks."

"*OK then*, Joel it is," Jay said with a smile as he walked out.

After getting dressed, they all went in different directions. Reid and Joel headed for the golf course, while Jay, Buck, and Stu walked towards the administration building.

• • •

Before they reached the golf course, Joel and Reid walked by a lacrosse game. They saw a player spin around his defender, dive over another, and while horizontal, take a mid-air shot and score a goal. Joel stopped in his tracks in complete awe. "Let's stay and watch for a few minutes. That was amazing. I've never seen anybody move like that."

"Now you know why lacrosse is America's fastest-growing sport."

They walked over, climbed the bleachers, and sat. Joel remained mesmerized as both teams scored goal after goal. "Makes me wish I played the game. My high school had a pretty good team. I ran track instead. You played high school lax, didn't you?"

"Yeah."

"I'll bet you were captain of your team."

"Co-captain."

"Must be nice to be the best at every sport you play."

"You don't have to be the best to be captain."

"Oh, come on, Reid, don't pull that modest BS on me."

"I'm *not.* Being a captain is not about being the best. It's about leadership and attitude."

"So you weren't the best on your team?"

"I didn't say *that.*"

Joel just laughed as Reid tried to act humble.

They turned their attention back to the game just in time to see an attackman feed the ball from behind the goal to the crease attackman. The man with the ball faked a shot and, in one swift movement, fired the ball behind his back as he spun past the goal. The goalie didn't even realize the ball had gone into the net behind him.

Joel stood and yelled, "Nice shot," a little louder than he intended.

Half the players looked over to see who was yelling. Some of them spotted Reid and waved their sticks or their gloved hands. Reid gave a quick salute and asked Joel, "Had enough yet? Can we go?"

"Do we have to?"

"Yes, we have to."

"It looks like they're coming off the field. Can we grab a couple of sticks and take a few shots before we leave?"

"Sure, why not," Reid said.

They walked over to the players who were on the sideline taking a break and asked to borrow a couple of sticks. As they grabbed two sticks one of the players said, "Why don't you take mine instead, Reid; you'll like it better than that one."

"Why?" Reid asked.

"Because I've trained it better than he has. Mine scores a lot more goals."

The statement brought on a lot of laughs, some jeers, and a punch from the guy who had given Reid his stick.

Smiling, Reid said, "Think I'll use the one I've got; I saw it shoot some great shots a few minutes ago. He winked at the owner of the stick, who gave him a thumbs up.

Reid and Joel spent the next ten minutes having a catch and taking shots on goal. When the players came back onto the field, they left for the golf course.

"Now that's a game I would have enjoyed," Joel said. "Why did you stop playing?"

"To make an agonizingly long story short, I had to decide between lacrosse, football, and golf. I couldn't play all three. There wasn't enough money in lacrosse so I chose football. I was pretty good till I got knocked unconscious in a college game. When the doctors warned that another blow to my head could kill me, I made the switch to golf."

"Obviously it was a good move."

"Yeah, I guess so."

They walked into the locker room and Reid got Joel a pair of golf shoes. They put on their shoes and went to the range. Five AllSport golfers were hitting balls. Reid watched and gave each a few tips as he walked by. After some quick stretching, he began hitting balls. One by one the others stopped hitting and walked over to watch, each hoping to catch something that might help them with their game.

Reid hit a few balls with each iron, then grabbed his driver. After sending ten balls straight as a laser beam to the far edge of the range, he turned toward the surrounding golfers.

"OK, here's the deal, each of you get one ball." He pulled a ball marker from his bag and handed it to the closest guy. "Mark it with your initials. The two farthest balls, closest to the center line, will play a round with Joel and me right now. Gentlemen, Carol," he added to the tall lean girl with sunglasses resting on the brim of her cap and a dark braid winding halfway down her back. "Tee up your balls and fire when ready." He made no exception to the rule for Carol who was known to regularly out drive most of the men at AllSport anyway.

She won along with a guy named Mort. Although her shot was not second in distance, it was a very close third and right on the center line.

The excitement of playing eighteen holes with Reid showed in Mort and Carol's eyes. The tips they would get from the world's top golfer could be invaluable to their careers. On the way to the first tee, Joel said, "I think I'll just walk with you three. I would just hold up your game if I played."

"Nonsense," Reid said. "If you're going to be tied to my side for the next few days, you may as well learn the game. I need to play at least eighteen holes a day in preparation for my tournament at Shinnecock in two weeks."

"If you say so, but no laughing please; I'm very sensitive."

"Ha, now that's funny," Reid said. "You sensitive—give me a break."

"Hey, I may be able to take down a man twice my size in seconds, but I still tear up every time I hear the line 'You had me at hello,' when I watch 'Jerry McGuire.'"

They all laughed.

Joel actually hit a pretty good drive on the par four, 300 yard, first hole. His ball landed just off the fairway about 180 yards out. Carol's drive was excellent, leaving a short sixty-yard chip. Mort-while longer off the tee, ended up in a bunker just in front of the green. Reid drove the green and two putted for a birdie.

It was a perfect day for golf. Not too sunny, not too hot, and just enough breeze to keep the players cool. The foursome walked the freshly cut grass of the second fairway, joking and laughing as they towed their pull carts.

19

Down in New Jersey, Leigh and Emma's search for Diane Powers had been challenging but somewhat fruitful. The good news: they were on her tail. The bad news: she knew it. After leaving the sanitarium, they went directly to her family's home. The family was outraged that she was a possible suspect. Diane's sister, Lynn, helped her avoid them by driving her to her best friend's home to hide. It took some serious convincing, but eventually Emma got through Lynn's head. Lynn had been the victim of an abusive husband; therefore, in her mind, even when innocent, the best way to avoid trouble was to run and hide. Using basic interrogation tactics, Emma persuaded Lynn to give up Diane's whereabouts. Leigh and Emma pushed their rental car to its limits. Motion detection lights came on as they drove into the friend's driveway. Emma pushed the doorbell on the small weather-beaten house. They heard a squeak followed by the slam of a door coming from the back of the house, and then they heard the growling and barking of an agitated dog. Leigh turned, grabbed the railing, and launched herself over the side of the steps. She landed and rolled after the seven-foot drop, before taking off running around the side of the house.

Emma was about to follow when the door opened. A young woman with her hair wrapped in a towel asked if she could be of help. Emma quickly asked about Diane. When the woman denied knowing her whereabouts, Emma turned, grabbed the railing ready to vault, then shook her head and ran down the steps, following Leigh.

Emma yelled out to Leigh, trying to get her bearings. Hearing Leigh's voice but not understanding her answer, Emma ran in its direction. Three fences and four backyards later, Emma found Diane lying face down in a flower bed with Leigh sitting peacefully on top of her holding Diane's arm twisted high behind her back.

After catching her breath, Emma asked, "Why didn't you let me know that you already had her? I nearly impaled myself on that second fence." Emma lifted her arm to show her torn shirt, or at least what was left of it.

"I did. I guess you just didn't hear me. I'm glad you're here though. You can bring this feisty bitch back to the car. Watch her though, I think she bites."

"What do you mean she bites? I'm not bringing her back myself. If you haven't noticed, she's a little bigger than I am."

Leigh rolled her eyes and said, "Fine, then do me a favor. Take off that shredded shirt and use it to tie her wrists and gag her."

"Take off my shirt? Are you crazy? I'm not taking off my shirt."

"Well, there's not much left of it anyway."

"Forget it, because I'm not doing it."

"You're such a wimp," Leigh kidded. "Take Diane's sweatshirt off her and put it on. Diane, do you have a shirt on underneath your sweatshirt?"

"No!"

Leigh was getting tired of the nonsense. "Oh, too damn bad." She twisted Diane's arm and said, "Get up." It took a harder twist to convince her but Diane finally stood up. She continued to fight as Emma tried to lift off her sweatshirt.

"Get the fuck away from me, bitch," Diane shouted.

"Could you please hurry," Leigh said tightly.

Emma nodded as she took off her shirt and ripped it in long strips. She folded a strip and tried to gag Diane from the front. Diane kicked her in the shin and continued to curse her out.

"Ow, you bitch," Emma said, finally losing her patience. She grabbed Diane's hair from behind and wrapped the gag around her head, tying it twice with force. Then with Leigh's help she pulled the sweatshirt off Diane, leaving her in just her bra. Emma immediately tied Diane's wrists behind her back with the remaining strips of her shirt.

"Holy cow, it's about time," Leigh said.

"Oh, shut up," growled Emma as she tugged the sweatshirt down over her body.

"Ready to go? You grab her right arm, and I'll get the left."

"I have a better idea. Give me the keys and sit on her again. I'll get the car."

"I knew there was a reason I liked you. You may be a wimp but you're always thinking."

"It wasn't that big of an idea."

"Well, if we had dragged her back, kicking and screaming, by the time we got her to the car you would have thought it was."

"Good point. OK, one for me." Smiling, Emma raised her hand and drew an imaginary vertical line in the air with her index finger.

"Emma?"

"Yes?"

"Can you please just get the damn car already?"

"Oh, of course." Emma turned and ran.

Leigh rolled her eyes again and called Emma back.

Emma came running. "What now?"

"These might help." She tossed Emma the keys.

"Right." She took off again.

• • •

Half an hour later, they were in the car discussing where to take Diane to interview her. Her parent's house was too hostile. The local police station would require too much red tape. AllSport was too long of a drive. They decided the car would have to do. They parked behind some stores in an unlit parking lot.

Leigh turned to Diane and said, "I'm going to take off your gag and untie your wrists. If you start to scream or fight, I'm just going to put them back on. We just want to talk with you. We can either do it nice and calmly or you can make it difficult. I promise you won't enjoy the difficult way. Do you understand?"

Diane nodded placidly. She had stopped squirming as they drove.

"Turn your head," said Leigh reaching for the gag.

As soon as it was out of her mouth, Diane said, "Ow, that thing hurt." She moved her jaw around to loosen it. "I promise to stay calm as long as you guys promise not to bring me back to that nut house. Please, please don't take me back there. I'm not crazy, really I'm not. You can't take me back. I don't want any more drugs. Pleeease." She was melting down in front of Leigh. Her pleas had become sobs.

"Shhhh," Leigh said, as she untied Diane's wrists. "We're not going to take you back. We just need some answers."

Diane slowly calmed down. Emma handed her a tissue and she wiped her eyes and nose. She looked at Leigh and asked softly, "Aren't you guys from the asylum?"

"No, we're not. I promise we're not here to take you back there."

"Then tell me what you want to know."

"Where did you go when you left the sanitarium?"

"Home."

"And where after that?"

"Nowhere. I've been at my parent's house the entire time. Why?"

"You really haven't gone anywhere?"

"No, I'm telling you, I've been at their house the whole time. I had to beg them not to take me back to the sanitarium. They wanted to, but I convinced them not to."

"Diane, tell me about Bob."

"That bastard! I hope that bitch of a wife is making him miserable. He was going to leave her and marry me, the son of a bitch. You know if anybody's crazy, it's her. She's nuts. You should have seen her when she caught us together. She went insane. I thought she was gonna kill me. She doesn't deserve him. He doesn't even love her. He loves me."

Leigh looked at Emma who was in the front seat looking back. Emma raised her brow questioningly. Either Diane was putting on a good show, or she had no idea that Bob was dead. It was time to change the direction of the interview.

"You must be pissed, Diane," Emma said. "I know if it was me, I'd probably kill the bitch or maybe even Bob. I mean if you couldn't have him, why should she?"

Diane's eyes grew wide. "Kill him? Are you crazy? I love him. I couldn't kill him." Her face twisted in thought. "I couldn't kill her either come to think of it. I couldn't kill anybody."

Emma and Leigh watched her closely as she said it. They looked at each other again and both nodded acknowledgment. It was time to be direct.

Leigh turned back to Diane and said, "Diane, Bob is dead. He was murdered."

"What?" said Diane. "Cut it out, don't play games with me."

"I'm serious, Diane, he was killed earlier this week."

Diane stared at Leigh silently, slowly realizing that she was serious. “No, nooooo,” she wailed, covering her face with her hands. “Oh no. No, no, no,” she sobbed.

They let her cry. Once again they looked at each other and, without saying a word, acknowledged their belief in Diane. They were both convinced. She didn’t kill Bob.

Leigh reached out and held Diane’s hand while Emma called Jay and explained the details.

20

Back at AllSport, Jay was in the middle of an interesting interview. Wendy Ross, one of the internal auditors from the accounting department, had returned from her ICSF audit in New York. As Jay spoke with her, she revealed two things: first, that a discrepancy had been found by one of the auditors from the CPA firm about a month and a half ago. The auditor had brought it to Bob's attention during a meeting Wendy had attended. And second, that Bob and Joe Spinelli had had a serious argument the next day.

Jay asked, "Why doesn't anyone else seem to know about either issue?"

Wendy said, "I figured the information about the money loss was in the right hands so I never mentioned it to anyone. The argument between Bob and Joe was after hours and behind closed doors. As far as they knew, no one had heard them. I didn't want to come off sounding like a busy-body so I kept it to myself, until now, that is."

"Do you know the name of the auditor?" Jay asked.

"Sure, it was Carlos Rodriguez. We worked together on audits regularly, at least until then. I haven't seen him since then."

"Since you worked with him, did *you* know anything about the lost money?"

"No, I only audit incoming donations. I match them with

deposit tickets and bank statements. Believe me, there's enough money coming in to keep me busy full time, actually more like time and a half."

"Who audits the outgoing money?"

"No one internally, just the accounting firm. There are no conflicts of interest that way."

Jay nodded. "Sounds right." He thought for a moment. "You say you haven't seen Rodriguez since that day?"

"No, I haven't."

"Isn't that odd? How often was he around here before that?"

"It seemed a little strange to me; he used to be here two, sometimes three days a week."

"Did they replace him? That is, before Bob changed accounting firms, did the old firm put somebody new on outgoing audits?"

"No, I think they started having everything faxed daily to their office in New York. The new firm works the same way. I'm sure it saves them a fortune in expenses."

"I guess that can work," Jay said with some doubt. "It seems to me it might be easier to hide things that way though."

"I agree," Wendy said.

"Hmm, I guess I'll have to follow up with Mr. Rodriguez."

"Probably a good idea."

Jay nodded. "OK, Wendy, what can you tell me about Bob and Joe's argument? Think hard, and I'm sure you can recall something."

Wendy raised her eyes in thought. She began to slowly shake her head. "I'm sorry, I knew they were fighting but I couldn't make out a single word."

"Can you remember who was louder or who sounded more defensive, anything at all?"

"No, nothing, sorry."

"You have nothing to be sorry about. You did great. In fact, you've given me plenty to follow up on. Thank you."

"Sure, no problem. Let me know if you need anything else, and I'd be happy to help. Bob was a great boss, by far the best I've ever had. I'm really going to miss him." After a brief silence, she said, "May I go now?"

"Yes, Wendy, you can, but do me a favor. Keep thinking about the fight you heard. If you remember anything, please let me know immediately, whether you think it's relevant or not."

"I will," she said as she stood. She shook Jay's hand and left.

Jay immediately placed a call to Stan Rosen at the accounting firm. He asked Rosen about Rodriguez. Rosen explained that Bob had requested that Rodriguez be dismissed, not from the account but from the firm. When Rosen had asked why, Bob said that he had argued with him and he was totally out of line. Rosen explained further that when he talked to Rodriguez and learned his side of the issue, suspicious thoughts about Bob had entered his mind. Rosen knew he had a double-edged sword in his hand. What if he blew the whistle on the CFO of his firm's biggest account and then found out the accusation was incorrect? The firm would lose the account, and that was out of the question.

But what if he bit his tongue and it was later found out that Bob was stealing money? What would happen if it was found out that he knew, and had remained silent? The final effect would be the same, and he'd be damned either way. The only thing that finally saved him from having to make the decision was that Bob fired the firm before Rosen had a chance to take action. Rosen, although devastated at the loss of the account, was totally relieved that the decision was now moot.

Jay was pleased to hear that Rodriguez was still employed by the firm. He asked Rosen if he could come down and interview Rodriguez personally. Rosen acquiesced without further thought.

Jay hung up his cell only to be told that Mench was waiting for him on line two.

He pushed the speaker button and said, "Hey, Mench, got something good for me?"

"No, sir. Greeny and I are coming back on the next flight. Bogota is a bust. Faxton's cousin, Juan, is a respected doctor down here. He's in the middle of a pretty serious malpractice suit at the moment, which explains most of that phone call that was overheard with Faxton. He laughed as he remembered the call. He said he could understand how it could have sounded incriminating, even cartel-like. He said they spoke about his court battle. His malpractice suit is due to a prescription he wrote that was misread. A pharmacist gave his patient the wrong drug, which brought on a heart attack and killed him. Then afterwards, the patient's widow came to his office and threatened him with a gun while cursing him out. In the end she broke down into tears and put the gun down. Hence, the use of the words: drugs, kill, and weapon. As for the use of Spanish, it's fairly common when two Latin Americans converse. Bottom line, Jay, the trip was a big waste of time. We'll see you soon."

"We got the same explanation of the call from Vasquez. All right, you guys should try to get flights back as soon as you can. Things are opening up here in a few directions. I could use your help."

"We'll get back as quickly as possible. Bye."

"Bye." Jay hung up, rubbed his face with both hands, and looked out the window, deep in thought.

Wispy clouds floated by, sporadically shading the bright sun. A crystal ornament hanging in the window reflected sunlight throughout the room in a rainbow of tiny beads of light. Staring at the crystal, Jay folded his arms and leaned back in his chair, his brain trying to sort out the overload of information it had taken in the last couple of days. Something didn't fit; something just didn't seem right. *But what*? A knock at his open door snapped him out of his reverie.

"Come in."

"Don't you look perplexed," Jody said as she walked in and took a seat in front of his desk.

"Yeah, I am. I just don't know what's bothering me. I'm glad you came in because we need to brainstorm. Will you take notes?"

She grabbed a pen and a pad of paper. "Fire when ready."

"Is Jake free or in an interview? As long as we're going to do this, he should be here too, so we can all catch up and see what direction we need to head in."

"We just took a break. He was going to get something to eat. He should be back in the boardroom by now."

Jay pushed the intercom button and paged Jake.

Shortly after, Buck entered the office, and right behind him was Jake. "I heard you page Jake," Buck said. "So I decided to be nosy."

"We're going to do some brainstorming," Jay said. "Make yourselves comfortable, gentlemen."

Buck and Jake each sat on opposite ends of an ugly, greenish, Naugahyde couch.

"Any of you mind if I light up?" Buck raised a cigar in the air that he had been carrying around all morning. "Helps me think."

"No, no problem, enjoy yourself," Jay said.

Buck glanced at Jody and Jake; neither objected.

As Buck torched his stogie, Jay began. "Well, I just had a very informative interview with one of the in-house auditors from accounting." He quickly recapped his interview with Wendy.

As he finished, he noticed both Jake and Jody had odd expressions on their faces. "What's up, you two? You both look confused."

"Jay, we just interviewed Brendon Scanlon," began Jake. "He's the other in-house auditor. He said that Wendy had been acting funny for a while. He noticed that she had been a little squeamish whenever she was near Bob or Joe during the past few weeks. I was going to tell you that we need to check *her* out. But I guess like every other investigation we've run, the more we dig the clearer things become."

"Duh," Jody kidded.

"Oh, shut up. You know what I mean."

"Yeah, I guess even that's becoming clearer now," she jabbed again.

"Guys, can we please get serious?" Jay said with a pleading look.

"Sorry," Jody said. "I couldn't help myself."

"Fine, now let's move on. Let's make a list of the people we need to follow up on and those that we've ruled out thus far. Let's start with those we've cleared."

"Karen Thomas is clear," Jody said.

"Diane Powers is clear," Jake said.

"Vasquez is clear," Jay added.

The others looked at him surprised. "Really?" Jody asked.

Jay quickly explained the phone call from Mench.

"Funny how information from one side of a conversation can get so twisted, only to be quelled by an explanation from the other side," Buck said.

They all nodded. "Let's continue," Jay said.

"Luigi, the artist, is clear," threw out Jake. "Chuck called in. The guy is very busy. He's making a fortune based on the reputation he earned from his artwork here. Teams all over the world are hiring him. He's been working in France for the last few months. Chuck confirmed his alibi."

"The Hunting Lodge owner is also clear," Jody said as she wrote.

"Faxton obviously didn't do it," Jay said.

"You can clear the two accountants from the CPA firm," Jake added.

They were all quiet as they continued to think.

"I think that's it, so let's start the next list. Put down our friend Edwin Riley," Jay sneered. "Add John Umeana too. Hopefully we can lock the two of them up later today and be done with this."

"What about Carlos Rodriguez, the auditor from the CPA firm?" Jake asked.

"Yeah, we need to go speak with him," Jay said. "I don't think he's a suspect, but maybe he can shed some light on the whole thing."

Once again they were all silent.

"Is that really it?" Jay asked. "You guys can't add anyone to this list? Come on."

Jake and Jody shook their heads.

"OK, Buck, you and I need to head to New York. Most of the partners at the CPA firm were hostile to my guys. Losing the account set the firm back serious money as well as hurting their reputation. I want you there in case we have to make some kind of peace offering in order to get information."

"Peace offering? What the hell are you talking about?" Buck asked.

"Truthfully, I'm not really sure. I just want to be prepared, OK?"

"It's your case, man. If you need me, I'm with you. When do you want to go?"

"I'd like to go now."

"All right, let me go grab a few cigars. I'll meet you down in the lobby. I want to get a golf cart and head out to the course to let Reid know we're leaving, OK?"

"Of course, I'll meet you downstairs in about ten minutes."

Buck left the room and Jay said, "I'd like you two to keep

interviewing. I feel pretty good about Riley being our man, but until it's confirmed I want you guys to forge on."

"Sure, Jay, you got it," Jake said.

Jay tapped the speaker button on his phone and dialed a number he found in his Blackberry.

Ringing from the speaker filled the room.

"Yeah, Jay, what's up?" Bill answered.

"Have you met with Umeana yet?"

"No. We're at DiGiacomo's club. Umeana is nowhere to be found. He was supposed to be here an hour ago but he never showed."

"Damn, I was counting on wrapping this thing up. Is anyone looking for him?"

"As a matter of fact, DiGiacomo is. He is so pissed off that one of his guys might be responsible for Bob's death, that he's put word out on the street that he wants Umeana brought in immediately."

"I wouldn't want to be Umeana right now."

"Me either."

"Hey, is Sal available? I'd like to talk to him."

"Let me check," Bill said.

Jay, Jake, and Jody heard background noises as Bill's chair slid against the floor as he got up. They heard knocking on a door. Next they heard Bill ask if he could speak with Mr. DiGiacomo. Two new voices could then be heard telling Bill to wait. Then they heard Bill say, "Come on, guys, you don't have to frisk me; I'm carrying in an ankle holster." They heard some shoving and then Bill's voice again, "You heard me, get your fuckin' hands off me."

Next they heard a bunch of noises they couldn't decipher, followed by a heavily accented voice saying, "Leave him alone, let him come in." They assumed it was Sal DiGiacomo.

"He's packin', boss. Let us just take his gun."

"I said, let him in. He's not gonna shoot me. He's one of Jay Scott's guys. Come on over and have a seat."

They heard some more odd noises before Bill said, "Sorry, Jay, I dropped the phone. Hold on, here's Mr. DiGiacomo."

After a second, DiGiacomo said, "Jay?"

"Yeah, Sal, it's me."

"Your man here is pretty entertaining. He just handled two of my best guys like they were amateurs."

"I'm not surprised; I choose my people well."

"I guess you do. What can I do for you?"

"I heard that you were annoyed that your man, Umeana, might have had something to do with Bob Thomas' murder."

"Damn right, I'm furious. Believe me, Jay, if he had anything to do with it, it will be his last job."

"That's why I wanted to talk to you. I need Umeana alive. My guys have to speak with him. He's no good to me dead."

"All right, Jay, you have my word. I'll make sure your guys get to speak with him first. I'll deal with him afterwards."

"Grazie, Sal."

"Prego."

Jay pushed the speaker button to hang up.

"Did he just imply what I think he did?" Jody asked.

Jay nodded.

"Will he do it?" she asked.

Another nod.

21

Jay met Buck in the lobby and followed him out to a waiting golf cart. Buck handed him a cigar and lighter and said, "Sorry, I must have dropped my cutter somewhere."

"No problem." Jay bit off the end and lit up. As they caught up with Reid and the others on the 14th fairway, Joel was just teeing off. His shot was a beauty, landing just in front of the green and rolling on. He couldn't hide his excitement as he turned to walk off the tee box.

"Nice shot!" Jay said. "When did you learn to do that?"

"Within the last hour. It seems this assignment has its advantages. Reid is teaching me his game, in trade for some martial arts training. You won't believe this; he actually asked if I could teach him Dim Mak."

Jay's eyes widened in surprise. He turned to Reid. "Dim Mak?"

"Yeah, is there a problem? I've been reading about martial art styles and Dim Mak sounds impressive."

"Do you even know what it stands for?"

"Not really; it just sounded like a good way to defend myself. You know, just in case."

"Reid, Dim Mak, which means Death Touch, is the ancient martial art of striking vital points in an opponent's body. It is used solely to cause death. Not many instructors even know the specifics about Dim Mak techniques. Those that do are reluctant to pass the knowledge on to their students." Jay looked at Joel. "Tell him the most interesting part."

"I was a martial arts instructor in the Seals," Joel said. "I specialized in Dim Mak. When you mentioned it, I thought somehow you knew and were playing games with me, testing me to see if I would teach it to you, which by the way, *I will not*."

"Interesting, I had no idea. I really just thought it sounded cool. Tell you what—the hell with Dim Mak. I'll let you choose the style. In fact, let's drop the whole subject for now; you have a makeable birdie putt to think about. Let's go, champ."

"Look who's calling me champ," Joel said with a laugh.

"Hold up a second, guys," Jay said. "We didn't come out here to watch you play, although I'm very impressed, Joel. Buck and I are heading to New York to interview the accounting auditor. We need to get a better understanding of some accounting discrepancies." Jay was being intentionally vague. He had no idea who the other two golfers were, and he didn't want to take the time to find out. "We'll keep you posted if we find anything new."

"Reid, come with me for a second," Buck said. Buck put his arm over Reid's shoulder and turned him around, leading him away from the others. "Are you doing all right?"

"I'm fine. Seriously, you don't have to worry about me. Just go to New York and find the bastard. I'll be OK."

"That's what I'm worried about. You've been strong. Maybe a little *too* strong. I'm worried that it's going to hit you all of a sudden. If it does, I want you to call me immediately. Shane or I will come back here right away. Don't try to handle this yourself."

"Thanks, I appreciate it. I've been talking to Shane a lot on the phone. I may seem tough to you on the outside, but I've been doing a fair amount of crying while I've been on the phone with her. Don't be fooled; I'm hurting inside—big time. Bob and I were friends since we were kids. We were actually walked together in strollers as babies. He was like a brother to me."

"Just call if you need me. I'll keep the chopper waiting, just in case. I can have it pick up Shane also. Just let me know."

"I will, Buck, thank you."

"No need for thanks. Hey, about the upcoming tournament, if you need to back out, it's OK. I already called Griffin and let him know what's going on. By the way, he sends his condolences."

Reid gave a disappointed look.

"What's the matter?" Buck asked.

"I really wish you hadn't called Greg. He's going to feel obligated as Commissioner of the PGA to inform the entire tour. I'm not ready for phone calls from everyone." He sighed, "Oh well, too late now."

Buck shrugged. "Sorry, I thought I was doing a good thing."

"Don't apologize; it *was* the right thing to do. I just have to prepare myself for the calls."

"When they start, just forward your cell phone to Nancy, so she can deal with the calls."

"Good idea."

"OK, we're going to take off. Do me a favor and find out whatever you can about the funeral. I want to inform the accounting staff and have a bus ready to take them down."

Reid nodded. "I'll find out from Shane and let you know."

• • •

Lance's cell-phone rang, just as he was about to take the first bite of his hot, overstuffed, corned beef sandwich. Damn, he'd had a hankering for this sandwich for hours. Frustrated, he put it down and grabbed his cell. After a glance at the caller ID, he pushed the speaker button and answered, "Yes, Mr. DiGiacamo."

A rough, garbled voice came over the speaker. "It's not Mr. DiGiacomo, it's...," a mixture of interference and marble-mouth made understanding the guy difficult.

"I can't understand you. *Who* is this?" Lance asked, cutting him off.

"Tommy Vio...," more interference broke up his voice.

"Tommy *who*?"

"I *said* it's Tommy Viola, like the fuckin' instrument, ya know." His attitude poured through the phone.

With a grin, Lance decided to play with the guy. "Hey, great name, I played the viola in high school. Is that how you got the name? Did you play it too?"

"Are you kiddin' me? No, I didn't play the fuckin' viola. Look, fugedabout how I got the name." More attitude. "Let's drop the freakin' small talk. Sally—uh, Mr. DiGiacomo, wants you to come back here now. He found Johnny Mean."

"Johnny Mean? I guess that's Umeana, right?"

"Riiight. Look, just come back already; Sally's waitin' for you."

"Fine. Tell Mr. DiGiacomo—uh, Sally, that we'll be right back."

After hanging up the phone, Lance looked at the others with another grin. "That was some conversation." He looked down at his plate. "Oh well, so much for my sandwich. Let's go." He picked up the sandwich and took a big bite. Closing his eyes, his whole face smiled in ecstasy.

"Pretty good, huh?" Keith asked. "Hey, I never knew you played the viola."

"I didn't, I was just playing with the guy. Can you imagine a wiseguy playing the viola? Wouldn't exactly be good for his reputation."

"So where do you think he got the name?" Beebs asked.

"If I had to guess I'd say he probably whacked a guy and stuffed him in a viola case."

"Nah, a viola case is too small for that. It's about the size of a violin," Bill said.

"Oh, I thought it was much bigger than that. What's the big instrument called? You know, the one that stands up on the floor?"

"You're thinking of a cello or a bass." Bill said.

Lance nodded. "I guess…Ah, who knows. Let's go see Uncle Sally." Lance took another bite of his sandwich and wrapped it up.

Keith chuckled. "Uncle Sally, that's good."

• • •

DiGiacomo's club was in the same neighborhood as Mario's restaurant. The four men squeezed into a cab for the ride to East Harlem.

The back seat wasn't big enough for Bill, Lance, and Beebs. Bill had to shift around to get his phone out of his belt clip. As he reached for the phone, his hand got a little too close to Lance for comfort.

"Sorry man," Bill said.

"No problem," Lance said. "I kind of enjoyed it."

Bill shot him a questioning look. Lance had a reputation as a womanizer.

"I'm kidding, dude. Can't you take a joke?" Lance asked.

Bill's skeptical gaze at Lance lingered.

"Seriously, I was kidding! Give me a break; you know me better than that."

"Come on, Lance," Beebs said. Tell them the truth. We've been lovers for years."

"What? Are you crazy? Shut up, you fool."

Keith turned and looked back in surprise. Bill and Keith were now staring at Lance and Beebs, wide-eyed in disbelief. Even the driver was looking at them through the rearview mirror.

"Beebs, you better tell them the truth, *now*," Lance threatened.

Beebs tried to keep a straight face. Finally he erupted in laughter. "All right, all right, I was just kidding. You guys know Lance well enough. I think last night at the hotel was probably the first night this year that he didn't pick up some babe. He may act it sometimes, but he's not gay."

"What do you mean, I act it?" Lance turned around and hit him hard.

To everyone's surprise the cab came to a screeching halt. The cab driver turned in his seat and demanded in a very effeminate voice, "Gentlemen, there will be *no* gay-bashing in my cab. Do you understand?"

"Gay-bashing?" Beebs said. "Oh, come on, we're just joking. Believe me, none of us have any problem with anyone's sexual preference."

"OK then," said the driver as he turned back and continued to drive.

They arrived at the club, paid the driver and stepped out of the cab.

As the car drove away, they all burst out in laughter.

A few moments later, they walked into the club for the second time that day. It was classic good guys versus bad. The bad guys were not accustomed to the nonchalance expressed by the intruders. In fact, they were offended that their wiseguy persona did not intimidate these four at all.

This time, obviously as per DiGiacomo's instructions, there was no pat down, which was an absolute first. No one ever approached DiGiacomo without being searched, especially when it was known that they were carrying. The tension on the side of the wiseguys could be cut with a stiletto.

The guys were ushered into Sal's office immediately. Another first. Visitors *were always* made to wait before seeing Sal.

Sal stood and motioned for them all to sit on the dated but

clean upholstered couches and easy chairs. An old threadbare Persian rug covered the hardwood floor. As they sat, a man in a waiter's uniform carried in a large silver tray with an espresso pot, demitasse cups, and spoons. The waiter reached for the espresso pot.

"I'll pour, Frankie," said Sal. "Be a good boy and go get us some nice pastries."

Without asking, DiGiacomo poured and passed espresso for everyone. He then picked up his own cup, sat back in his chair, and took a sip. "Gentlemen, I'll get right to the point. As they say, I've got some good news and some bad. The good news is that we found Johnny Mean. The bad: he can't meet with you. He's dead." He looked at Lance. "It's not what you think though. He died in a car accident out in Montauk."

"Mr. DiGiacomo, you think there was any foul play involved? I'm not implying you were involved but maybe someone tinkered with his car? Do you know anything about the accident?"

"All we know so far is he crashed on the beach."

"On the beach?" Lance stared at Sal while tapping his fingers on the arm of his chair. "Nothing's ever easy, is it, Sal?" he said with a heavy sigh.

"I'm afraid not, mi amico."

Lance turned to the others. "Well, unless any of you have any better ideas, let's get going. Next stop, Montauk. Anybody have a surfboard?"

They all stood, thanked DiGiacomo, and turned to leave. As they were walking out, the waiter entered with a tray of mouth-watering Italian pastries. Keith and Lance stopped to take a look. They glanced at Sal who said, "Take em, take em all. You'll love them; they're outta this world." He raised his hand to his mouth, closed his eyes, and kissed his fingertips in a gesture of gastronomic appreciation.

Lance took a cannoli and Keith a mini Napoleon. Biting into

his pastry, Keith couldn't refrain. "Oh, my God, this is fantastic," he mumbled with a mouthful. He turned to Sal and gave him a thumbs up.

"I know, they're good, also a little messy," Sal said pointing at Keith's chest. "You might want to get yourself a new shirt."

Keith looked down to see a glob of custard on his shirt. "Oh shit," he said as the others all laughed.

"There's a men's clothing store across the street," Sal said. "Tell Steve, the owner, that I sent you."

Out on the sidewalk, as they waited for Keith to buy a shirt, Bill called Jay and explained their new dilemma.

He hung up and said, "Beebs, will you hail a cab? We're gonna go to Montauk by chopper. It's down at the helipad on the lower East Side."

• • •

As Jay and Buck were led to Stan Rosen's office by a very plain-looking brunette receptionist, they could almost feel the chill of the stares they received from the partners they passed. Rosen's office was large and fairly comfortable but rather stark. The off-white walls were bare except for a few diplomas and CPA certificates. Loose papers were strewn amongst piles of books and stacks of manila folders. Rosen sat behind a large cluttered desk that had a picture cube in one corner and a letter opener with a golf ball at the end next to it. On the other corner was an overflowing in/out basket. The only semi-clean area in the office was by a wall where a green felt strip laid with a golf ball return machine plugged in at one end and a putter leaning against the wall at the other.

"Please excuse the mess, gentlemen; I'm on the road most of the time so I don't spend much time in this hell hole. Would you like something to drink; coffee, Coke, water?"

Jay and Buck sat in two straight-back, upholstered chairs.

"Coffee would be great, thanks," said Jay.

"Same here, thank you," said Buck.

Rosen pushed the intercom button on his phone and said, "Sarah, could you bring us three coffees?"

"Yes, Mr. Rosen," she answered with an edge.

He looked up and shrugged. "Sorry, you guys are not very popular around here at the moment."

"So be it. Thanks for seeing us so quickly," said Jay.

"I don't really think I had much choice. If I let you wait in our reception area, it could have been dangerous for you." He smiled. "I say that in jest of course."

"Of course," Jay said unamused. "Look, we didn't expect a warm reception here; maybe we should just interview Rodriguez and leave. We certainly don't want to upset anyone any further."

"Buck, let me ask you a question. I'm fairly certain Jay will solve this crime soon. When he does, I'm sure you will find everyone at this firm innocent. If that's found to be the case, would you consider rehiring us? After all, we have never had any problems before this. Have we?"

"Let's see where this all ends up before I offer anything. But I will promise that if it is proven that no one here had anything to do with Bob's murder, then we will consider hiring you back."

"Fair enough, that's all I can ask. Thank you."

"OK," Jay said. "Where should we meet with Rodriguez, here or someplace else?"

"Hold on a second. I'll call him and have him meet you in one of our boardrooms." He picked up his phone and paged Rodriguez. "Hi, Carlos, it's Stan. Carlos, Buck Green, and Jay Scott are here to speak with you. I'm going to bring them over to Boardroom One. Will you meet us there?" He listened. "Thanks, see you in a minute." He hung up the phone.

"Come on, gentlemen, follow me." They walked through a

maze of hallways to a boardroom. As he passed a girl sitting at her desk, speaking on the phone, he said, "Thanks for the coffee, Sarah."

Sarah's reaction was priceless: a mixed expression of embarrassment and anger. Buck and Jay couldn't help from laughing.

Carlos was already seated at the table when they walked in. Like everything else in the offices, the boardroom was very plain. A few certificates on the wall, a large veneer table, and a mixture of straight-back, upholstered chairs and metal folding chairs. Everything was low budget. The firm was either cheap or they wanted to portray efficiency and give their clients the impression that they were not overcharging them.

Carlos rose to shake their hands as he introduced himself.

"Carlos, I'd like to thank you for meeting with us. I'm sure you know the importance of this discussion. What you reveal may help us find Bob Thomas' killer."

"I hope I can help. I really don't believe I know anything relevant, but I will certainly answer all your questions."

"Very good. Well, let's get started." Jay turned towards Rosen. "Stan, I hope you don't mind if I ask you to give us some time alone with Carlos."

With a look of surprise, Stan responded, "What? Oh. Sure. OK—I guess." He stood and slowly made his way out the door.

Buck got up, closed the door, and went back to his seat.

"Carlos, can you tell me how long you worked on the ICSF and AllSport accounts?" Jay asked.

"I guess it's been close to two years."

"Did you always have the same assignment?"

"No. When I started I worked as a general auditor. After about a year I was given the more specific job of auditing all accounts payable."

"Were there others who worked on it with you?"

"Absolutely. Do you know how much money flows out of that place? Sorry, dumb question, of course you know. It's not possible for one person to do that job."

"Where did you spend most of your time—at AllSport or here in your office?"

"I spent three days a week at AllSport, then one day at Mr. Green's office working on the overall ICSF account, then one day here in my office."

"Where did you stay when you were up at AllSport?"

"In campus housing where I had a little apartment."

"Who did you work with most of the time?"

"Mostly the people in accounts payable. Sometimes with Mr. Thomas and pretty regularly with Mr. Spinelli."

"And what exactly did your job entail?"

"I audited all expenditures and compared them to the banking and brokerage statements."

"What was the majority of the money spent on?"

"Payroll, maintenance, construction, travel, food, I could go on and on."

"Now, Carlos, we were told that you found some serious discrepancies. Can you tell us about them?"

"Sure," he thought for a moment. "Well, every once in a while we pull random checks that have been cashed. We call the company they were written to, just to verify what work or service had been performed for the payment. Some of the companies I called weren't calling back, even after I had left several messages.

"I didn't think much of it at first, but after a while I became curious. At first I wondered why answering machines or services answered the companies' calls all the time. But when I thought about it, I realized that it's pretty common for start-ups or small companies without a large staff. In fact, sometimes our firm recommends the use of an answering service to our clients. It's much less expensive than a receptionist."

He took a sip of the coffee he had brought in with him.

"Anyway, my curiosity intensified when I called one of the companies and realized the voice on their answering machine message sounded very similar to that of another of the companies. I called them both a few times and although I couldn't identify the voice, I realized they were definitely the same person."

"Interesting," Jay said.

"Yes, I thought so too. So the next thing I did was print out a statement of all checks written to these two companies over the past year. One had been paid about $275,000 and the other about $340,000."

"Really, over half a million?" said Jay.

"That's pretty common. AllSport has quite a few accounts that get paid much more than that."

"Really?"

"Sure, millions are spent on food, travel, and construction and maintenance every year. AllSport feeds, houses, and flies an awful lot of people around the country."

"I never really thought about the costs associated with all of it," Jay said, looking at Buck.

Buck nodded. "Guess it's enough to kill for."

"Maybe." Jay turned to Carlos. "Let's get back to the issue at hand. Tell me more about the checks."

"They were all printed on your dedicated printer and all stamped with Bob's signature. All very common. Every check was below ten grand, therefore needing only one signature. Further research proved that all the checks written to the companies in question were fairly similar in size and all were deposited at the same branch of the same bank. The total amount was just shy of four million dollars." Carlos took another drink of his coffee.

"What did you do with this information?"

"I went to Bob with it."

"And?" Jay asked.

"He asked me to keep quiet about it and let him figure it out. Actually he told me if I discussed it with anyone he would fire my firm."

"Didn't he ask the firm to fire *you*?"

"Yes, eventually he did, but originally I guess he figured he was better off with me remaining on the account. He was pretty sure that he was safe as far as I was concerned."

"That had to be difficult information to keep to yourself. What did you do?"

"What could I do? I was damned either way. At first I gave him a few days, then asked if he'd come up with anything. He told me he was working on it and that I should just continue doing my job and let it go. When I told him that it *was* my job to find these errors, he became angry. He said it was my job to find errors and report them, and since I had done that already, I should leave the investigating to him."

"I guess that stirred some suspicions?"

"Uneasiness is a better description. At that point I kind of understood why Bob wanted to keep things quiet. Letting something like this out of the bag could crush ICSF and AllSport. I mean, as soon as word gets out about money being stolen from a charity, incoming money practically comes to a halt. Would you give money to a charity if you knew that four million dollars had recently been stolen from it?"

"Absolutely not. Very good point, Carlos. Tell me more," said Jay.

"Well, let's see." Carlos tilted his head up, furrowed his brow and chewed on his lower lip. "I gave him a couple of weeks before approaching him again. This time when I asked how his investigation was going, he kind of blew up. He yelled at me, saying if I couldn't leave it well enough alone then I was done, off the account. He threatened that, if I mentioned anything to anyone at the firm, he would make sure I was fired. That's when I'd had enough of his crap; I retaliated by saying that they wouldn't fire me for this. I was just doing my job. In fact, by not telling them, I was way out of line. Misappropriation of four million dollars is no small issue. The auditing CPA firm needs to know. The police need to know. The Feds probably need to know too. Then, as I started to walk out, he threatened that if I said a word to anyone he would give the firm the option of firing me or losing the account."

"You must have been mad," Jay said. "I know *I'd* be pretty pissed off if someone threatened *me* like that."

"That's an understatement! I was furious. That son of bitch was threatening me when it should have been the other way around." Carlos face had reddened.

Jay just looked at him.

"Wait a second, what's going on here? Are you thinking that I had something to do with this? Are you crazy?"

"Well?" Jay raised his brow in question.

"Why the hell would I jeopardize my life and my family by doing something that stupid? Look. Just take a look at me. What do you see? I'll tell you. You see a nerd, a pencil pusher, a bean counter. I was picked on throughout my entire childhood. Even my family makes fun of me for being a wimp. You know what? I wish I had the balls to do something like this. Ha, what a joke!"

"I've seen stranger things happen, Carlos," said Jay.

Carlos gave Jay a very troubled look. "Do I need an attorney?"

"Do you?" Jay asked.

"I don't believe this. I've done nothing wrong, except maybe keeping this information to myself for too long."

"Carlos, if you're innocent, you have nothing to worry about. If you're guilty though, I'll nail you."

"This is insane. I swear to you, I'm innocent. I agreed to come to talk to you to help you solve this crime. Now you think I did it? This is ridiculous."

"Let's hope so, Carlos. Thanks for your time; you've been a big help."

"Yeah, right," he said in disgust as he stood. "I'm going to say it one last time before I leave." He turned and faced one man and then the other as he stated calmly, "Jay, Buck, I had nothing to do with this. I swear." He walked out and slammed the door.

Buck looked over at Jay. "So, what do you think? Do you really think he could be our guy?"

"Nah, I just went with the flow of the interview. He made it too easy. Did you notice, I didn't raise the question of his guilt; it was all him. Once he got started he couldn't stop. It's common in interviews. People get so nervous they read way too much into our questions."

"So you were just playing with him?"

"Maybe a little, but I *have* cracked cases under similar circumstances when the interviewee blurted out an unexpected confession as part of a nervous reaction."

"So what's next?" Buck asked.

"I want to get back to AllSport. I let Bill and the guys use the chopper to go to Montauk. They have to investigate a car crash. I have Chopper II coming to get us. We need to get back and follow up on some arguments."

"Arguments?" Buck questioned.

"Yeah, I've had something bothering me for days but I couldn't put my finger on it. Well, Carlos made me recall my interview with your in-house auditor Wendy. She mentioned that Bob and Joe Spinelli were arguing about something. I want to find out what it was."

22

Near the summit of Mount Everest

Clink. The sound of the ladder shifting caused Joe Spinelli's entire body to tense as he crossed over what seemed to be a bottomless crevasse. Sweat forming on his brow trickled into his eyes, in spite of the icy, minus-ten degree, howling wind, causing temporary stinging blindness. Having already slipped, his body lay prone, hugging the horizontal ladder fiercely. Never before had he experienced such a gut-wrenching fear. He only had five feet of ladder left to cross; it might as well be one hundred.

What kind of idiot am I? he thought. *I'm a freakin' CPA and here I am climbing Mount Everest like I have something to prove, and paying a fortune to do it.* He knew the ladder had looked too rickety to cross. Why, for once, hadn't he listened to his inner voice, the one that told him not to be the first in the group to cross the deep void? Why? Because he never listened to that voice! If he had, he would be somewhere else on vacation right now. Somewhere sane, like a beach maybe, or even skiing. His last vacation of extreme skiing seemed like a cakewalk in comparison to his immediate situation.

He pulled his body another few inches and the ladder shifted again. "Shit," he screamed as fear surged through him. If he didn't get to the other side quickly, the ladder would surely give out. He had to wipe the thought from his mind. He didn't want to die.

Not yet. Life was just becoming fun. He had plans to travel the world and tackle every adventure imaginable. He had to get across. He slowly bent his leg, placed his foot on the next rung and pushed hard. The force was too much for the frozen metal ladder. It snapped in two, dropping both itself and Joe into the frozen abyss. Joe closed his eyes as he dropped; he barely felt the tug of the rope as it became taught and swung him into the icy side of the crevasse. He slammed into the wall once, hard, and bounced, then dangled for a moment before he realized he was tethered by a lifeline to those above him who had yet to cross.

Dazed from hitting his head against the ice wall, he barely heard the calls from above as the Sherpas slowly pulled him up. Mentally drained from the near-death experience, and physically exhausted from both the bitter cold and the difficult climb, Joe felt them raise him while his body dangled like a dead man's. As he was pulled up, he slowly lost consciousness.

Minutes later, after his team had dragged him out of the crevasse, they huddled around him in silence, thinking he was dead. Blood that had trickled from his hairline near his temple was quickly coagulating as it froze. Lying on his back with a peaceful look on his partially frozen, blood-drained face, his eyes suddenly sprang wide open. Some of the group let out a gasp of relief, while the Sherpas just laughed.

23

Although in Jay's mind, things were pointing heavily towards Umeana and Riley, he needed to figure out what was behind the argument between Bob and Joe Spinelli. It bothered him that Spinelli was conveniently out of town with no possible way to communicate. Coincidence or plan? As far as Jay was concerned, coincidences were rare, *extremely* rare. Before he and Buck landed back at AllSport, he had called Jake to request a thorough search of Spinelli's office. It was difficult to investigate a crime when the people you need to question are either out of reach or dead. Umeana's death was already going to add a layer of difficulty in pinning him and Riley to the murder. Now, without Spinelli around, how was he going to investigate the argument?

Did Spinelli find out about Bob's theft of ICSF funds? Did they argue because Joe threatened to blow the whistle? Jay was not happy that Spinelli wasn't due back for another week. Obviously, the Sherpa who had set out to give him the message had not accomplished the task.

The only thing left to do was dig through Spinelli's and Bob's offices and residences. For Joe's home, they would need a warrant. Jay made the necessary calls.

The office search so far had revealed nothing. Jay decided to search Joe's computer and a cell phone that was on his desk. Jay called Art Fornham and asked if he could send over AllSport's technology guy.

Two minutes later there was a knock on the open office door. "Come in," Jay said.

"Hi, I'm John Doyle, the Information Technology Director. I'm better known around here as the computer guy. Art told me you need me for something."

Jay stood to shake his hand. "Nice to meet you, John. How'd you get here so quickly? I only called Art a minute ago."

"My office is only one floor down. They like to keep me and my team close in case the network goes down."

Jay nodded. "Well, I'm glad you're here. I'm going to need some help with a few things."

"I'm all yours."

"First, can you get one of my guys into Joe's computer? We can't get past the password."

"That's what it's there for," John said with a hint of sarcasm.

"Excuse me?"

"I'm sorry, Mr. Scott. Of course I'll get you in."

"Thank you. By the way you can call me Jay."

"OK, Jay, and you can call me JD."

"Good. My next request may be a little more difficult. Can you get me the records of any phone calls or emails Joe made or received during the last month and a half?"

"Sure, tell me what you need: date, time, phone number, address, email address?"

"You can get all that?"

"No problem. It'll take a little while but we'll get it done. I guess you wouldn't mind recordings of the phone calls too?"

"That would be excellent." Jay rubbed his chin in thought. "Any chance you can get me into his voicemail? I'd like to listen to his messages."

"Yeah, sure. Do you want what he's listened to or just the ones that he hasn't heard yet?"

"Wow, all of them would be great."

"All right, I'll have Anthony come in and get you into his system. I'll get to work on the phone stuff."

"JD, sorry to double your work on this, but can you get me all the same information for Bob too?"

JD pursed his lips and clucked his tongue while slowly nodding, obviously deep in thought. "Yeah, I guess. It's going to take some time though."

"I'll be here."

As JD left, Dave Wheeler walked into the office.

Jay looked up. "Hey, Dave, how are you?"

"Pretty good. You?"

"I'm OK. We're definitely making headway. Still some loose ends but we're narrowing them down. Have anything that might help?"

"As a matter of fact, yes. After we found the car at the airport, I put a couple of my people there to follow up. After checking the airlines we found that someone actually flew out of the airport using a ticket with Bob's name on it."

"I'll be damned."

"I know, it doesn't seem to make any sense. Why the hell would they try to make it look like Bob took off, if they were just going to dump his body out in the open for us to find?"

"Beats me. So what else have you got?"

"The ticket was for a connecting flight to Caracas, Venezuela. My guys reviewed the airport security tapes and found a pretty good image of the guy. It took a while but they were able to use a tape from the boarding gate. Two hundred-thirty people boarded, so the process of elimination took some time.

The picture we got is fairly good. It was enlarged into a poster, and it's being posted with a reward everywhere throughout Manhattan and the surrounding boroughs. My buddy, Alex Garcia, is a captain in Harlem, and he said we should start getting calls immediately and probably have an ID within and hour or two. If not, we'll ask the Feds to run it through their database."

"Good," Jay said, nodding. "Hey, if you want to stick around, I could use some help."

"Sure, what can I do?"

"I've got phone records and recordings as well as an email log for both Bob and Joe Spinelli coming to me soon. It's going to take some time to dig through it all."

"Spinelli? Why do I know that name?"

"He's the Director of Accounting. He's been away for about a week and isn't due back for a while. Turns out he and Bob had a pretty serious argument before he left."

"What kind of argument?"

"We're not sure yet, but it was just after an auditor found that a bunch of money was missing from AllSport's account."

"Missing money, huh? This thing is taking some interesting turns, isn't it?" said Wheeler.

"It's the usual, right? Why do people usually get wacked? Drugs, money, sex. Never changes, never will."

Wheeler nodded his agreement.

Jay looked at his watch. "Eat lunch yet?"

"No."

"Come on, let's go grab something while we're waiting."

24

Lance's friend, Doron Brates, met the helicopter at the Montauk Downs Public Golf Course. The course was the easiest and most convenient spot the pilot could find to land. The parking lot had been full of cars so they landed on the tenth fairway, disrupting the golfers.

The four men jumped out of the chopper. Lance and Beebs tipped their caps at the foursome on the green, who were standing there dumbfounded.

After a quick jog to the parking lot, it was easy to spot Doron's big red van. They got into the vehicle and Lance introduced everyone. The van was a ten-seater.

"Doron, I didn't know you drove a bus," kidded Lance.

"With five kids and three dogs, this thing *just* fits us."

The men all chuckled.

"So, my friend, I guess you want to go see the crash site?"

"You know about it?"

Doron started to drive. "*Know* about it? *Everyone* knows about it. It's not everyday we have a Porsche drive down one of our beach access roads at close to eighty miles an hour. He hit a pile of sand that had been dumped the day before to help stop some of the flooding we've been having. I didn't see it, but I'm told the car must have flown about twenty feet before nose-diving into the rocky beach and rolling over. The guy didn't stand a chance."

As he drove the van down Ditch Plains Road he said, "Here we are."

He parked and they all got out. The parking lot was filled with cars, vans, and SUV's all with surfboard racks. Surfers in wetsuits were everywhere, walking with their boards to and from the beach, or sitting on their tailgates tugging wetsuits on or off. The men followed Doron to the end of the lot. Police tape cordoned off the regular walking path to the beach. Just beyond the tape there was a large pile of sand with tire tracks going up the side.

They walked around the edge of the cordoned off area and continued alongside the tape down to the beach. Ducking under the tape, they walked to a big hole in the sand.

Bill looked back towards the mound of sand that had acted as the take off ramp. "That pile is about six feet high, and we're about eight to ten feet lower than its base. A car taking off at around eighty would probably add another ten feet to that. Wow, a nose dive from twenty-five feet up. There's no way he could have survived that."

"Excuse me," yelled a surfer from just outside the yellow tape. "You know that tape is here for a reason. You're interfering with a crime scene."

Bill walked over and explained who they were. The surfer introduced himself as Hubie Van Meurs.

Bill thought for second and repeated the name, "Hubie Van Meurs, why do I recognize your name?"

Hubie said, "You said this investigation has to do with All-Sport, right?"

"Correct."

"Well, you must have been on the investigation team when Reid had gotten the death threats a few years ago."

"Correct again."

"You guys checked me out back then. Reid and I were business partners in a golf course deal a long time ago. The deal went bad and he and I and some other partners each lost a lot of money."

"Oh yeah, I do remember that. One of the partners killed himself, right?"

Hubie nodded.

"So, Hubie, what do you do now? I mean when you're not surfing, that is."

"I sell."

"What do you sell?"

"Home performance and remodeling."

"Home performance?"

"Yeah, we help homeowners reduce energy costs; you can check it out at alure.com. Well, if you'll excuse me, I'm gonna go hit the waves." He ran off towards the water.

Bill turned and walked back to the others. "Hey, Doron, would you happen to know where the car is?"

"Probably at the police station."

"Can you take us there?"

"Of course, let's go."

"One second, I want to watch that guy ride a wave," Bill said.

They watched a couple of surfers catch some waves. Then Hubie caught his. He was a big guy and rode the wave effortlessly, catching air and doing floaters as he milked the wave for all it was worth.

He obviously knew Bill was watching, because when Bill gave him a thumbs up after his ride, Hubie returned the surfers' hang loose sign or Shaka, as it is known in Hawaiian.

• • •

At the police station, the guys learned that the Porsche was, in fact, owned, driven, and crashed by John Umeana. They also confirmed that he was found dead inside the car. The crash had broken his neck, not to mention a variety of other bones in his body. He had been wearing a wetsuit, obviously on his way to surf.

When they inquired about the car, they were told it was being examined at a local service station. They boarded the van and drove down the street to the station.

The owner, a retired cop, slid out from under a car on his mechanics dolly and stood. He wiped his greasy hands on a soiled rag as he approached. He was wearing a grease-stained, gray, mechanics jumpsuit with the name Rick embroidered over the left breast.

"Gentlemen, they told me to expect you. I suppose you'd like to see the car?"

"We would," said Beebs.

Rick waved them around the back. "Follow me."

As they turned the corner they saw the wreck. The front end of the black Carrerra looked like an accordion. The windshield was not only smashed, but you could see the curve where Umeana's head had made impact and pushed it out. The inside of the windshield and the dashboard were washed in sticky crimson.

The rear hatch was propped open revealing a bright, immaculately kept engine. Rick nonchalantly pointed in the direction of the engine.

"There was definitely tampering involved. The brake line was cut and drained and there was a device attached to the throttle mechanism. As soon as the car was put in drive, the throttle was immediately opened to maximum. You don't see many of these babies with Tiptronic shifting; this thing must have taken off like a rocket."

"What's Tiptronic?" Bill asked.

"It's an automatic transmission. Kinda takes the fun out of driving a Porsche. Don't you think?"

Bill nodded. "So, if the gas was set to hit full throttle as soon as it was put in drive, the tampering must have been done here in Montauk, sometime before he got into the car to drive to the beach. Right?"

"Had to be. Word has it, he was staying at a house right down the road from the beach. I was told he was a wiseguy, which explains some of the toys I found in the car."

"Toys?"

"Come, I'll show you." He led them back into his office. "I was gonna take these back to the station after I closed up. I figured they'd be safer in here for now."

He opened a closet door while pulling a clean rag out of his pocket. He leaned over into the closet and when he turned he was holding a scratched, hard plastic case. He placed it on his desk.

"This was on the floor behind the driver's seat. Looks like it got banged around some in the accident." Then removing an over-burdened key chain from his belt, he leaned over, unlocked and opened a desk drawer. He pulled out a Sig Sauer P229 and placed it next to the case. "That was strapped under the seat."

"Mind if I ask you to open the case?" Beebs asked.

"Sure, no problem." He reached and opened the case with the rag.

Three of the guys just whistled.

"Wow, would you look at that," said Lance. A Walther WA2000. You can't get one of those for less than about forty grand."

The rifle was magnificent. Highly polished, fine-grained wood surrounded the black steel firing mechanism, barrel and oversized scope.

"You'd have a hard time even getting one at that price," remarked Beebs. They only made about seventy of them."

"We're going to have to get this to the lab immediately," Bill said, looking at Rick.

"If Captain Gorman says you can take it, it's all yours. Let me call him." He picked up the handset on an old black rotary phone and dialed.

After a quick conversation he hung up and looked at Bill. "No problem, guys; he just wants you to sign a receipt for it."

They signed a grimy, oil-stained piece of paper which acted as a receipt for the weapons, then thanked Rick and left.

After a quick call reporting their findings to Jay, they were directed to bring the guns to a ballistics lab in New York City. The same lab was already examining a slug that had been found outside the deli where the hit probably took place.

25

Jay Scott was torn; he had narrowed the case down to just a few strong possibilities. First, he had John Umeana and Ed Riley. Riley's motive of revenge was strong; incriminating evidence was piling up against him. If Johnny "Mean's" weapon matched the slug found outside the deli, then the case was closed.

Then there was the second possibility; he wanted to see where the recordings and email trails were going to lead them. What was taking Doyle so long? Jay's patience was dwindling. He desperately wanted to call JD and push him a little. Problem was, he knew when he applied pressure to someone other than his own team, it usually backfired. When Jay Scott pressured people, they tended to get very nervous and potentially careless, making their findings less than acceptable. Hence, he waited.

While waiting for information was irritating, it was also a good time for thinking. He asked Buck and Reid to take a walk with him.

Before they left the building, Jay had explained the Montauk car crash, and while doing so he expressed some excitement as he talked about the surfing. Reid then intentionally led the walk towards the aquatics area. As they approached, the distinct crashing sounds of a waterfall grew in their ears. They had been discussing Reid's decision whether to play in the upcoming tournament or not.

Curiosity finally got the better of Jay and he asked, "What's that sound? Don't tell me there's a waterfall here."

"No, Jay, no waterfalls." Reid pointed to a warehouse-sized building across the walkway. "That's the Surfer's Oasis, one of the few man-made surfing facilities in the world."

"Are you really going to tell me there are guys surfing in there?"

"Come on. Let's go in," said Buck.

The roar of crashing waves muffled the background noise of the machine that created them. The pool was enormous. Its surroundings were designed to simulate a beach with a sandy-colored shore, a real wharf, and a craggy rock jetty. Tremendous fans on the sides created the true feeling of a windy day. The biggest difference was that the smell of salt air was replaced by that of chlorine.

Video cameras on tracks and cables followed surfers as they rode. The men walked over to a woman who was standing at what looked like a podium.

"This is Toni Rothschild," Reid said over the noise. "Toni's the director of our surfing program. Toni, I'm sure you know this is Jay Scott. Can you tell him a little about the facility?"

"I'd be happy to." She turned to Jay, "Well, Mr. Scott, our facility is the finest of its kind, but I'm sure that doesn't surprise you. As with all the venues on campus we have the top professionals in the country training our athletes here. Over there," she said, pointing to a man and a woman studying a video monitor, "are Andy Irons and Rochelle Ballard, both world champions."

She turned and pointed to a large blue door. "Behind that door is the wave machine or, Swell Master, as we like to call her. She can create all the main types of waves which allows our surfers to practice in conditions similar to those they'll come across in competition. One of the things that make surfing such a challenge is that every wave is different. The way they break drastically affects the type of wave.

"First, we have the Beach Break. It's where the waves break on the sandy seabed. This type of wave is the best to start surfing on. Next, we have the Point Break—There was a movie named after it! The Point Break is a wave that breaks onto a rocky point. Finally, there's the Reef Break, which is a wave that breaks over a coral reef or a rock seabed. These waves are usually the classic ones that you see on surfing videos. They can be unforgiving if you happen to wipe out badly, but they are the most rewarding in their perfection. There's also the Rivermouth which can break over rocky ledges or sandy bottoms.

"If you look closely at the bottom of the pool you can see the false bottom. It can be raised or lowered. There are also ridges down there that we position like reefs. We can create a pretty realistic simulation of most of the competitive surfing sites throughout the world."

Just as she finished, she glanced at a surfer spinning at the crest of a huge wave. They all turned to watch as he masterfully spun his board, but then instead of continuing his wild ride, he was flung high into the air and landed hard on his face at the bottom of the wave. The gut-wrenching smack made everyone grimace.

Loud "Oooh's!" came from various parts of the building. Everyone watched tensely as the churning water rolled past the surfer leaving him bobbing face down in the water. Slowly he raised his head and gave a shaky scuba diver's OK signal which helped abate everyone's concern.

Toni let out a quick gasp of relief before continuing, "That demonstrates one of the benefits of practicing here versus over a real coral reef. Not only can the intense impact of the fall get you, but the chances of getting severely cut up on a reef are very high."

The surfer climbed out of the pool near Toni. "Hey, man, nice ride," said Reid. "Quite an ending, but nice ride nevertheless."

"Dude, you think that was hot, you should have been here yesterday!"

The statement brought a chuckle from everyone. Jay watched curiously as Toni adjusted levers and turned switches. The pool settled to a more manageable state of steady waves and the fans increased to a much higher velocity.

"What's going on?" Jay asked.

"It's windsurfing time," explained Toni. "We share the pool, each taking three-hour shifts."

Three windsurfers had been waiting at the edge of the pool and were already in the water, catching air on the waves. Jay was wide-eyed after watching one do a flip, board and all, and land perfectly. Buck said, "All right guys, let's get out of here. Thanks, Toni."

"Jay, feel free to come back when you've got the time to give it a try.

"Thanks, Toni, we'll see," he said as they left.

"You know, I love this place," Jay said as they walked away from the building. "I get an education every time I visit one of the venues, and all the thoughts and confusion temporarily get washed from my head. Where in the world, other than here, can you…."

Jay was cut off mid-sentence as about a dozen cyclists whizzed past them at breakneck speed.

"You were saying, Jay?" Reid kidded.

"I think you guys know what I mean."

Reid and Buck nodded.

"All right, let's get back to reality," Jay said. "I want to recap all our open issues. It helps me when I verbalize them and it will bring you both up to date."

"We're all ears," said Buck.

"All right, first, I've got a couple of my guys, Brooks and

Rosseland, heading down to Caracas to track down the guy that flew using Bob's ticket. As soon as we have an ID from the picture that's being posted, I'll forward it to them.

"Next, we have ballistics running tests on Umeana's gun and the slug we found, which, by the way, if I haven't told you already, we found outside the deli. Whoever removed the body missed it when he cleaned the area. They must have used a pail of water to wash away the blood. It left a trail as it found its way off the sidewalk and into the sewer."

Reid winced.

"I'm sorry for being so graphic, Reid."

"It's all right." Reid rubbed his face and sighed.

"Anyway, if the bullet and rifle match, we're done, yet if they don't it doesn't mean that Umeana couldn't have used another gun." He shook his head in thought. "There's nothing I hate more than a dead suspect. Like proving guilt isn't difficult enough."

"I hope Doyle has everything ready," Jay continued as Reid opened the door to the administration building. "It's going to take a while to research the calls, and then listen to all the messages and conversations."

• • •

Doyle was seated at the table as they entered the boardroom. Lined up on the table were duplicate sets of various things: piles of what looked like phone logs, cell phones, and machines that must be audio recording devices.

"I guess you're ready for us, huh, JD?" Jay asked.

"Everything's here." He pointed to each area explaining, "This is Joe's office phone log. This one's his cell log. This is a printout of all his email, both received and sent from two separate addresses we found. This digital recorder has all his office conversations and voicemail messages ready for playback and this one has his cell phone messages." He pointed to the other side of the table. "You've got pretty much the same over there for Bob."

"Excellent, thank you. Can you stick around to help us listen to these?"

"Of course I can; I was hoping you'd ask. I can't wait to hear this stuff."

"Just understand that what you hear may have to be kept under wraps for a while."

"No problem, I understand."

Jay picked up the office phone and called Jake on the intercom. "I'm in the boardroom with Reid, Buck, Joel, Stu, and John Doyle. JD's got everything ready for us. Can you gather Lisa, Wheeler, and two others and come in? We've got some tedious digging to do."

As he put down the handset, his cell phone chirped. He looked at the caller ID and answered it. "Go ahead, Bill." He listened. "Damn, it figures. OK, I'll tell you what, I want you guys to split up. Send Lance and Beebs out to Umeana's home or wherever the hell he was living and search for any other weapons. Call DiGiacomo first and let him know; he'll probably offer some kind of help. Go ahead and accept it because I may need him later so I want to keep him happy.

"I want you and Keith to head back to Ed Riley's place. It's time to put some pressure on him. I want to know where those missing rifles are. Have some fun with him, nothing too harsh but make the arrogant bastard sweat a little." As he hung up, the others arrived.

While they took their seats, he explained the phone call. Umeana's rifle and the slug did not match.

He then split everyone into pairs and gave instructions. JD gave a quick explanation of the recording systems. Four of the teams adorned headsets while the others sifted through piles of phone logs and email massages. As per Jay's instructions, reverse chronological order was to be used. As green highlighters streaked across pages and switches were flipped on and off, Nancy Baron's voice came over the speaker-phone in the middle of the table.

"Sorry to interrupt but there's a call for Chief Wheeler."

"One second, Nancy," Lisa said. "He's got a headset on." She reached over, tapped Wheeler on the shoulder and pointed to the phone. He pushed a button on the machine in front of him and pulled off his headset.

"OK, he can hear you now," said Lisa.

"Chief, Captain Garcia's on line two."

"Thanks," Wheeler said, picking up the handset and pushing a button on the phone. "What's up, Alex?"

After a quick conversation he hung up. All eyes in the room were on him, waiting.

"Believe it or not Garcia got an ID on the picture already. Name is Frank Stehlik. He's got a pretty long sheet and belongs to a Harlem street gang called Slam."

Reid, Buck, Jay, Joel, and Stu all flinched at the name.

"What's the matter?" asked Wheeler.

"The guy who had put the hit out on Reid was a member of Slam," said Jay. "Damn, we talked about this as a possibility, but the evidence kept pulling us in different directions." He looked at Joel and Stu. "I want you two to fly down to Harlem now. I want to be ready as leads come in."

Joel and Stu nodded and stood to leave. Joel walked over behind Reid who was noticeably shaken by the news.

He put his hands on Reid's shoulders and gave him a quick comforting massage. "I know you've heard this before, but try to stay calm. We will get whoever's responsible for this."

Reid took a deep breath, looked up at Joel, and nodded with a worried look.

As they were walking out, Jay said, "I'll call you as soon as we have anything new." He then picked up the phone and called for replacements to help comb through the paperwork. He was disappointed; once again, just as he felt they were getting close, new evidence sent them in yet another direction. He sighed in frustration.

"Come on, let's get back to work; I want to plow through this mess quickly."

26

The look on Barbara Riley's face sent a chill through Bill and Keith. She had already bitched them out before buzzing them through the driveway gates. Bill actually studied her hands before walking in. He was convinced that if she was carrying a weapon, she would have used it on them.

"I don't know why you're here and I *really* don't care, but if you're not out of here in half an hour I will personally throw you out. I have guests coming for dinner in an hour and I don't feel like explaining any of this nonsense to them. If you want to speak with my husband, he's downstairs. I'll send William to escort you." She turned her back on them and started to walk away. "Remember, I said half an hour," she added loudly, without turning around.

"Sweet woman," Keith said with a shiver.

"Yeah, just the kind you want to bring home to Mama," Bill said with a chuckle.

They heard a laugh behind them and turned to see the butler standing there chuckling. "Gentlemen, if you'll follow me I'll show you down to the shooting range."

They rode the elevator down. As the doors opened, shots could be heard coming from behind the closed door of the firing range. Bill took a few steps to the door and yanked it open without any warning.

Between shots, Ed turned to see who had just entered. "Hey, who the fuck do you think you are, barging in here while I'm shooting?"

Bill walked over and got right in Ed's face. "I think you need to put the gun down, Ed."

"Oh, now you're gonna start giving me orders, huh?" Ed lowered his handgun but did not put it down. Johnny had stepped out of the gun cleaning room, wondering what the yelling was about. The butler was standing by the entrance.

"Put the gun down, Ed. *Then* we'll talk."

"You know there's only one thing I dislike more than someone barging in while I'm shooting. That's someone who does it and then gives me orders, especially in my own house." Ed waved the gun around, without really pointing it at anyone. "You wanna talk to me? Then change your tone and your attitude, young man. Now get out of my face."

Bill had lost his patience and with a lightning fast maneuver, disarmed Ed with one hand and grabbed his fist with the other. He squeezed Ed's knuckles and bent his wrist back until he whimpered in submission.

"Sorry, Ed, but I have a hard time talking to someone who is waving a gun around me, and, as far as attitude goes, I think yours is the one in need of an adjustment. Now I'm going to put your gun down and then I'm going to let go of your hand, but only if you agree to calm down and answer our questions. OK?"

Ed just glared at him without answering.

Bill applied more pressure and tilted Ed's wrist further until he fell to his knees, wincing.

"Well?" Bill said, increasing the force.

Ed's brow was beaded with sweat. His eyes bulged in a mixture of pain and fury.

"Stop being a fool, Ed. If you'll just agree, I'd be happy to let you up. Give up the bravado bullshit and talk to me."

Ed stared at him for another few seconds, then groaned, "OK."

After Bill let go, Ed repeatedly flexed his fingers and rubbed his hand. Then he pulled a handkerchief from his pocket and moped his sweaty forehead.

Bill allowed him to settle down and asked, "You OK?"

Ed nodded in shame.

"Well, I'm sure you didn't expect things to backfire like they did, but I'm not sure I understand why you would chance going back to prison just for some childish revenge. I mean your life here is pretty good. It certainly couldn't get any easier. Too bad it's all over."

"Over?" said Ed. "Not for me. I didn't do a damn thing. If you're talking about killing Bob, well that's fucking nonsense."

"Sure it is. Then start explaining. First tell me why the van used to cart the body was in your garage?" Bill had no evidence to prove this but he wanted Ed to squirm a little before he asked the tough questions.

"The only van in my garage is the maintenance van for my property. It hasn't gone anywhere in weeks. Go take a look for yourself."

"Well, I can't exactly do that right now because if you didn't notice, the van was taken away on a flatbed to the forensic lab for testing. We'll have enough evidence with that alone to put you away for a long time."

"Do as you please; you'll find nothing incriminating."

"I'm glad you're so sure of it."

"Damn sure," said Ed.

"OK then, how about giving me the whereabouts of the two Brown Precision Tactical Elites. Let's see, I bet we find at least one at John Umeana's place."

Ed looked perplexed. "Why the hell would I give that rat-bastard my guns? He was the one who was gonna get guns for *me*. The son of a bitch hasn't even returned my calls lately."

"You're expecting him to call? Well, I wouldn't hold my breath if I were you. You see, Johnny Mean isn't so mean any more. In fact, he'll *never* be mean again."

"Are you saying that he's...."

"Yeah Ed, he's dead, very, very dead. Now, you may think that could be good for you, right? I mean if he's dead, then obviously he can't confess and he can't rat you out."

Ed just stared at Bill.

"Your problem is that there's another thing that a dead murderer can't do. He can't cover up the evidence. We're going to find the guns. We're gonna link him to you. Then we're gonna prove that you put the hit on Bob. It's over, Ed."

"Why don't you two follow me," Ed said to Bill and Keith with an air of renewed confidence. He led them out of the range and into the gun collection room. He walked to the far side and pointed at the wall. "Are those what you are looking for?" On the wall, filling in the empty outlines, were the two Brown Precision Tactical Elite rifles.

"I don't know, are they? Or are they replacements you've come up with since the last time we were here?"

"Oh, will you give me a break already. Do you know how difficult these are to get? They are the same guns that were up there before. Tell them, Johnny."

They all looked back at Johnny. He was wide-eyed. Slowly, he shrugged his shoulders and quietly said, "I'm sorry, Mr. Riley, but I haven't touched those since you put them up."

"Well dammit, Johnny, check 'em now. Go ahead and match the serial numbers to our records."

Johnny looked at Bill questioningly.

"Forget it, Johnny, it's irrelevant anyway. All I care about is that they were missing at the time of the shooting. Johnny, do me a favor; go get some gloves and the cases for the rifles. We're going to borrow them for a few days."

Bill waited for Ed's reaction, hoping he would put up a fight. Teaching him a lesson would be an absolute pleasure.

"Ed, I'll tell you what, you should go on up and get ready for your guests. We are going to do you a favor and get out of here before they arrive. If I were you, I'd stay in the house till we check everything out. I'm sure you noticed that you have visitors out on the road watching, just to make sure you don't run. Running would be foolish, Ed. It will make you look guilty and sometimes we can get trigger-happy when we think someone guilty of conspiracy to commit murder is trying to run away."

"Conspiracy to commit murder?" Ed growled.

"Shut up, Ed. Now come on up and see us to the door so we don't have to deal with your sweet wife."

Johnny handed over the rifle cases that he had carefully packed while they were talking. They rode up the elevator and walked out the front door to their car with Ed at their heals.

"Good bye, Ed, and oh yeah, enjoy your dinner; it'll probably be your last as a free man."

"Fuck you, this is all bullshit. I've done nothing wrong. It's all a big fucking coincidence: the guns, the van, Umeana. You'll see." Ed's face was red with rage as pushed the driver's side door closed, just missing Keith's foot.

"That's right, Ed, we will see, won't we?" Keith said as he drove off, spraying Ed with gravel.

Bill called Jay and reported in. Jay told him to bring the weapons straight in for a ballistics match. After dropping off the guns, he wanted them to meet up with Joel and Stu in Harlem and wait for further instructions.

27

The investigation had broken wide open up at AllSport. Jake had been listening to Joe Spinelli's cell phone messages. What he heard made him jump out of his seat. "Holy cow! You're not gonna believe this. Listen!"

JD removed the headset from the machine and plugged in some speakers. "Do I need to rewind it?" he asked Jake.

"Yeah, just a little; you need to replay the last two messages. Hurry."

JD pushed a button and watched the lights on the system blink. He pressed another button and a voice came over the speakers.

'Yo, man, you need to call me immediately. The deal has changed a little. The price of the hit has gone up. I want another fifty grand. That means you owe me seventy-five instead of twenty-five. Sorry, dude, but that's the way it is. You can pay it in two payments: another twenty-five K before the hit then fifty after. Call me so we can set up the transfer. Same as the first payment in small bills: tens and twenties. You know the deal.

'By the way, if you don't think I'm serious, you're wrong. If I don't hear from you soon, there will be a change in the program. We're still gonna take him out, but then you have a choice. Pay us what we want and we will dump the body as planned. Or don't pay us the extra money and we will dump the body where it will be found, and an anonymous call will be placed tying you to the hit. Your choice, my man. Call me.'

Different reactions of surprise circulated the room.

"Wow," said Buck.

"That son of a bitch." Reid was seething.

"OK," said Jay. "Now we have something to work with. JD, can you figure out where the call came from?"

"The number should be listed right on the caller ID list. If not, we can check the call log. Let me see that phone."

He flipped the phone open and asked Jake, "How many messages have you listened to already?"

Jake looked down at the legal pad in front of him. "There were three before that one, or after, if you want the order they came in. One of the other messages was from the same guy. You should play that as well. There was only one message in between them."

JD turned the machine back on and pressed the button. A female voice said, "Hi Joe." JD pushed another button and the machine squealed, then stopped. The next voice was the guy. "Hey man, I hope you took my last call seriously. You better call soon or things are gonna get pretty rotten for you."

Jay's mind was on fast forward. "OK, folks, now things are gonna get interesting. JD, I need you to figure out the phone numbers that match those calls. I want the rest of you to buckle down and dig up more evidence. I want to hear any recorded conversations between Spinelli and Bob. I want to hear all suspicious calls or emails to and from Spinelli, immediately. I want to know when he's due back, what flights he's on, and from where."

JD blurted out, "Here are the numbers. Actually it's the same number for both calls. It's a two-one-two number," he said as he wrote it down and handed it to Jay.

Jay handed the note to Wheeler who radioed it in to his shop and made the request for a reverse directory check.

"I've got something," Lisa said as she pushed a button on the machine she was listening to. A conversation between Joe and Bob started to play:

"It's you, isn't it?" accused Bob.

"What are you talking about?" said Joe.

"Look, don't play games with me. If you want to stay out of jail, it's time to fess up. I know how much the accountants say is missing, but I want to hear it from you. How much did you take?"

Joe was quiet.

"Joe, it's over, face it. Now tell me how much."

"A little over two million," Joe said sheepishly.

"Two? They told me it was more like four. Don't bullshit me, man. If you want my help, you need to be honest with me, totally honest."

"Honest? Bob, what the hell is honesty going to do for me now? Do you think I'm a complete idiot? Like I'd just waltz into your office, write down a confession, and *do the next ten years in jail*. No way."

"Calm down. Look, if you return the money, I'll get Reid and Buck to agree to be lenient. Maybe we don't even have to bring the law into this."

"*Lenient, ha that's a good one*. When was the last time Reid Clark was lenient? He doesn't put up with anything from anyone. He wouldn't be lenient on his mother!"

All eyes moved toward Reid, who just shrugged.

"Typically I'd agree, but this is different. ICSF's reputation is at stake here. If word of missing Foundation money hits the news, contributions will come to a halt. No one will give money to a charity where insider theft has occurred. If the only way to get the money back, and keep the situation away from the press is to go easy on you, he will."

"I'm not so sure. I need some time. Give me a few days; in

fact, I'm going on vacation in a couple of days. I'm going to be climbing Everest. It'll give me time to think. When I come back, either I'll walk right into your office with the money, or you can do what you need to do. What do you think?"

"I don't know. I'd rather get it over with now."

"Well, that's not going to happen. What are you worried about? Do you think that I'd stay in Tibet or Nepal? Not me, man. They're nice places to visit, but I'm too into my creature comforts to live with Sherpas and yaks. Look, let me just take this vacation, one last hurrah. Then I'll be back and I'll hand over the money and deal with the consequences."

"All right. Fine. Go climb the damn mountain. I'll be waiting when you get back. Make my office your first stop. Just understand one thing; if you run, we will come after you. I'm not sure if you know Jay Scott, but there is not a place on earth where you can hide from *him*. I promise you that Reid and Buck will spare no expense to find you if necessary."

"I get the point. I'll be back. Will you keep this to yourself until I return?"

"Of course I will. I have to. Can you imagine what they'd think of me if they knew I let you go, knowing about all this?"

"I guess you're right. Thank you, Bob."

"Just don't disappoint me, Joe."

The conversation ended and Lisa pushed the stop button.

"Looks like Spinelli's our man," said Jake.

"It certainly seems so. I know it seems cut and dry, but until he's in custody, I want to continue on the Riley, Umeana trail as well. We'll pursue them, Slam and Spinelli and see how it all pans out. Everybody please continue searching and listening to the recordings; I'm going to make some calls."

After Jay walked out, he dialed Lance on his cell. "So, what do you have for me? I hope something good."

"Well, this guy was a sicko all right. He's got a freakin' arsenal here. I'm talking guns, knives, explosives, you name it. There's also a ton of drugs and more porn than I've seen in my life, and you know me, Jay."

"Yes, I do. It must be an impressive collection."

"He must have been dealing the drugs. He's got enough pills and other stuff to get an army high. The porn collection is pretty remarkable too. There are magazines, video tapes, DVD's. Lots of sex toys and video equipment too. He must have been making his own stuff."

"Would you mind just telling me about the weapons? Is there a matching sniper rifle?"

"Oh right, sorry. Well, there's enough explosives here to take out most of Afghanistan."

"*Lance*."

"Oh yeah, sniper rifle. Well, how about everything but: he's got handguns, automatics, shotguns even a Tommy Gun, but not one stinkin' sniper rifle."

"How about ammo?"

"Plenty, and yes even some calibers that would fit a sniper rifle. Full boxes, half empty boxes, and a bunch of loose rounds and shells."

"All right, take everything that's a possible match and bring it to the lab, OK?"

"Ten-four, jefe. Adios."

Jay smiled and rolled his eyes as he hung up. Lance was good at the job but he was always such a clown. Well, it never hurts to laugh, does it?

Jay had been hoping that the phone call would have narrowed things down one way or the other. Instead it seamed that every lead was creating yet another.

He dialed Rosseland down in Venezuela. "Hi, Steve, anything yet?"

"Yessir, were about to go in and get Stehlik out of a bar in downtown Caracas."

"How do you know he's in there?"

"A lot of people know him down here. He lived here till just a few years ago. He left back then out of necessity. He had testified against some guy in a murder trial and a few people weren't very happy about it. I guess he either feels that it's safe for him to come back now or he's just testing the waters. Anyway, give us a few minutes...."

Rosseland stopped midsentence as the sound of gunshots came from within the bar.

"Oh shit, call you back."

• • •

As Rosseland and Brooks ran into Malabar, a trendy designer bar, it was as if they were swimming against the current. Scantily clad, gorgeous Venezuelan women poured in the opposite direction, screaming as they ran.

Once inside the chic establishment, the men forced their way against the path of the mass exodus to a terrace. Past the trees and bubbling waterfall, they came upon a small fish pond that was already turning into a diluted blood bath. A guy was lying face down in the murky water. Brooks grabbed him by the ankles and dragged him out of the water. With a quick shove, Rosseland turned the body over revealing two bullet holes in his chest. It was Stehlik.

They looked at each other amidst the pandemonium and simultaneously said, "Shit."

Brooks quickly pulled a wallet from the guys back pocket. Rifling through the contents of the wallet, he pulled three forms of ID each with Stehlik's picture but different names.

Both men stood to leave before the police arrived. Taking a

step towards the door, their path was blocked by two ugly over-sized goons.

Rosseland quickly flashed a badge at them. Then Brooks and he tried to continue on their way. The goons stepped in their way. One of them grabbed Brooks and said, "No tan rapido, caballero."

"Suéltame!" Brooks said, trying to shake the man off.

Rosseland looked at Brooks and said, "We don't have time for this; you ready?"

Brooks responded with a nod.

"Now," yelled Rosseland.

With a quick jab to the throat followed by a knee to the groin, Rosseland's opponent fell with a floor-shaking thud.

Brook's man, in spite of similar moves, was not giving up so easy. He had Brooks in a headlock and was squeezing hard when Rosseland hit him in the back of the head with a tequila bottle. Brooks managed to get out of the way as the oaf crumpled to the floor next to his friend. Brooks caught his breath, moved his head up, down, then from side to side, making sure everything still worked. Once satisfied, he smoothed out his clothes and joined Rosseland walking out as if nothing had happened. Rosseland caught Brooks taking a quick look in a mirror as they passed. As Brooks tried to stop and comb his hair, Rosseland grabbed his arm, pulling him away and said, "Not now, you clown. You never cease to amaze me."

"Come on, did you see all those beautiful women running by?"

Rosseland just shook his head as they exited the bar. They turned the corner just as a police car screeched to a halt in front of the entrance.

Rosseland reported in to Jay.

• • •

Hanging up the phone as he walked back into the boardroom, Jay looked down, shaking his head in disgust.

"What's the matter?" Buck asked.

"Another dead body, another dead end. That was Rosseland, one of the guys I sent to Caracas. They found Frank Stehlik, the guy who flew down using Bob's ticket. He's dead. He was in a bar with a couple of bullet holes in him."

Jay sighed. "Maybe if we keep this up all the bad guys will just get themselves killed. Now that would be the ultimate revenge for Bob." Jay's frustration showed as he rubbed his face then crossed his arms.

"Hey, cheer up, listen to what we just found," said Jake. He pushed a button on the recording machine.

"Speak," a gruff voice said, answering a phone call.

"Is this Victor?" came Spinelli's voice.

"Who da fuck's askin'?"

"Someone who wants to make you a sweet offer," said Spinelli.

"Talk."

"How would you like to make fifty grand and get revenge at the same time?"

"Revenge for what?"

"The Morgan brothers."

"Go 'head, you got my 'tention."

"Well, I know that Joe Morgan was a member of your gang, Slam. I also know he and his brother are in jail for attempting to kill Reid Clark."

"Keep talkin'."

"I've got fifty large for you if you'll kill Reid's best friend."

Silence.

"Are you there?" asked Spinelli.

"Uh huh. Jus thinkin'."

"Thinking's good."

"What, you bein' a wiseass, mo'fo? You don' wan' be no fuckin' wiseass wit me," he said quietly and slow.

"No, not at all. Seriously, I'm just glad you're thinking about it."

"Course I'm thinkin' 'bout it. Fifty large! Thad be fuckin' sweet."

"So do we have a deal?"

After a moment of silence, Victor said, "Yeah, you got yourself a fuckin' deal."

"Good. Now we need to talk about the specifics. You'll get half the cash up front. I will be leaving it in a duffel bag for you. The hit has to take place up near AllSport. You know the camp, right?"

"Gimme a break; every fuckin' athlete in the country knows AllSport. I used to go watch Joe when he played there."

"Good, then you know the area, right?"

"Some."

"Well, I need you to write down these instructions. You got a pen and paper?"

"No, hold on." He came back a few seconds later and said, "OK, shoot." Realizing what he said, he laughed, "That was pretty fuckin' funny, right?"

"Yeah. Ok, this is how it has to go down." Spinelli spoke slowly, giving Victor time to write. "Bob goes to the Wooden Nickel deli for his coffee everyday around six a.m. It's at the corner of Route 78 and Witherbee Avenue. Bob always parks in the same spot on Witherbee. There is a three-story apartment building across the street with a fire escape in the alley. Use the fire escape to go up to the roof." He paused. "You with me?"

"One sec'. 'K, go on."

"There will be a black duffel with half the cash near the wall where you'll take the shot from. I want you to shoot him before he goes into the deli. Then I want you to dump the body. I don't care where, but I don't want it found. Ever! OK?"

"No prob. What about the rest of the green?"

"When you're done and the body is gone, you'll call me at this number." As he heard the number, Jay looked at Jake who tapped on the legal pad in front of him indicating that he had already written it down.

The recording continued, "I will then tell you where to pick up the next duffel containing the rest of the money."

"Cool."

"Good. Last and most important: I want this to happen next Wednesday. If by some chance he doesn't show, then be ready again to do it on Thursday."

"What if he don't show then?"

"Never happen. He goes to the deli every day. He might miss one day, but no way he'll miss two in a row."

"Whateva you say, man."

"OK, if he doesn't show then just keep going back till he does."

"Cool."

"Good," said Joe.

"We done?"

"Yes, I guess we are."

"Peace out," Victor said with an evil chuckle.

The recording ended.

"When does Spinelli get back?" Jay asked.

"He's due in at three p.m. tomorrow."

"Finally, we have some *good* timing. Lucky we listened to this stuff today. Dave, I think we need to handle this quietly. I don't want to spook Spinelli and create a situation at the airport. You need to keep all uniforms out of sight. I want only plainclothes

officers and we should wait till he is out of the boarding tunnel and well into the building. I don't want him running back into the plane and taking hostages. I'd like to approach him first, and then you'll have your men move in as soon as I give them a signal. We'll keep it easy; I'll cross my arms when I'm ready for them to move in. OK?"

"Works for me," said Wheeler.

Jay dialed Joel and explained the recording. Joel agreed to call back as soon as he had any information on Victor.

In the meantime, Jay called Lance and Bill, and pulled them off their investigations.

28

Six two-man teams of plainclothes officers joined Wheeler and Jay's team at the airport. They had dispersed throughout the arrivals building. Spinelli's flight had already landed and had taxied to Gate 3. Jay watched the small crowd as they exited the tunnel. He almost didn't recognize Spinelli as he finally emerged. His hair was a mess, he had a scruffy beard, and his backpack would have made any normal man keel over. He walked past the gate security guards giving them a slight nod. Jay fell in place walking behind him and followed him through the terminal to the baggage claim area where Jay adjusted his stride to catch up.

As soon as he was walking next to him, Jay said, "Hi, Joe, my name is Jay Scott; we need to talk. Would you mind walking over this way and having a seat with me on that bench?" He nodded in the direction of a bench against the wall.

"Sorry, man, I don't know what this is all about, but I have to get my bags and catch a cab."

"Well, Joe, it's really in your best interest to speak with me. We can either do this the easy way or we can start making your life miserable right now."

"What the hell are you talking…."

A shot rang out and Joe grunted as he fell. Screams emanated from every direction and pandemonium broke out throughout the building.

People were running to hide behind anything they could find. Others were dropping to the floor covering their heads with briefcases or carry-ons. All at once about thirty cops, both uniformed and plainclothes, were in the area with guns drawn. Another shot blasted. More screams. A body fell from the steel grid structure overhead. As the shooter's gun hit the floor, it fired another round, hitting a woman in the shoulder. More screams. Another shot ricocheted off an overhead steel beam. Suddenly bullets were flying throughout the terminal. A plainclothes cop was hit. Another body fell from above, his automatic spraying bullets wildly as he dropped through the air.

Jay watched the disaster unfold from behind a concrete column with his gun drawn. Innocent travelers were getting hit by stray shots. Two uniformed cops were down. He reached for Spinelli's neck and found a weak pulse. He looked up, scanning the steel girders for any other shooters. No one that he could see. As his head turned, his eye caught the small flash of a gun firing from within a baggage chute. After a quick survey of the area, he dashed and took cover behind another column within firing distance of the chute. After another flash from the chute, a piece of the column just in front of Jay's head shattered, spraying concrete chips and dust into his face and his left eye. Putting aside the stinging irritation, he took aim with his right eye and fired two shots into the chute.

The eerie silence that followed gave Jay a moment of skeptical relief. Was it over? Were any of the shooters still alive? How many others had been shot? How many cops? Civilians? How many were dead? As these thoughts raced through his head, he heard a loud voice across the room.

"Drop the gun," an officer yelled. "Drop it now, punk."

All eyes watched as the shooter, a young kid wearing a black hooded sweatshirt and jeans, stared back at the cop. You could tell the kid was thinking of his odds. As he started to raise his gun, obviously preparing to shoot, the three surrounding officers all fired. Luckily the kid's trigger finger did not have a chance to squeeze off a round as he flew backwards, landing on the moving baggage carousel.

When the shooting stopped, cries and moans were heard from different areas in the baggage claim area. Just as Wheeler was about to give the all clear, an ear-piercing buzzer went off, sending everyone for cover yet again. Sighs of relief were heard once everyone realized it was only announcing oncoming baggage. As the machine started, the first thing to be dropped onto the conveyor was the dead body from the chute. It was a bloody, gruesome sight.

Wheeler gave the all clear and paramedics who had been waiting at the doors ran in and started treating the injured.

Jay's eye was bothering him as he walked over to the paramedic working on Spinelli.

"Is he gonna make it?" Jay asked.

"Yeah, he's lost a fair amount of blood, but it looks like he'll survive."

"Doesn't really matter anyway," Jay said. "Cause he's gonna get the death penalty after all this." Jay looked around the room. The EMT looked at Jay with a curious look.

"He caused all this," Jay explained as he stood.

Jay walked past other EMT's; some were loading injured civilians on stretchers, and others were working on police officers.

Jay approached Wheeler. "How are your men?"

"Don't know yet."

"Any of the shooters alive?"

Dave took a deep breath and said, "Yeah, two, barely." He pointed to two different areas where paramedics and cops had surrounded injured shooters.

Jay walked over to one of the groups, rubbing his eye as he walked. "Scuse me," he said. "I need to talk to him."

A paramedic who didn't know Jay said, "You can wait. We need to work on this man."

Jay wasn't in the mood to be diplomatic. "Don't start with me, young man. That filth you're working on just killed a bunch of civilians and police officers. Now step out of the way so I can ask him some questions before the asshole dies."

The EMT held his ground. "Look, I don't know who you are and I really don't care. This man needs my attention now and it's my job to give it to him. You'll get your chance to question him later, if he survives."

Jay's good eye grew wide with fury. Luckily, before he lashed out in anger, one of the cops let the EMT know it was OK.

Reluctantly, the paramedic stepped back and the others made room so Jay could kneel down and get close enough to speak with the dying man.

"I'm going to ask you simple yes or no questions, and if you don't answer me I will keep the medics away as you slowly bleed to death. Do you understand?"

The man slowly nodded, but his eyes were glazing over, more closed than open.

"No nodding. I want a yes or no to every question. Understand?"

The guy nodded.

"Say yes," Jay seethed.

"Yes," he slurred almost imperceptibly.

"Are you and the other shooters all members of Slam?"

"Yes."

"And you came here to kill Spinelli?"

"Yes."

"Because he owed you money?"

"Yes."

"Money for killing Bob Thomas?"

"Yes."

"So you guys killed Bob?"

Silence.

"I asked you a question, punk. Do you want to slowly bleed to death right here?"

"No."

"Then answer my question. Did you guys kill Bob Thomas?"

"Yes."

Jay stood and said to the paramedic, "*Now* you can save him…or better yet, *not*."

The EMT went back to work immediately.

Jay walked back to Wheeler and told him what he had heard. Then asked, "Do you have a count yet?"

Dave nodded with his eyes closed. "Yeah," he said with a quiet sigh. "Three officers: one dead, shot in the head. The other two are pretty bad." He paused, taking a deep breath. "Four civilians: one dead, two critical, and one with a superficial wound. There were five shooters including the one you spoke with, the other four are dead." With his head hung low and eyes wet, he looked at Jay. "What's with your eye?"

"It's nothing, just some crap that got in it from a close shot."

"You need to get that looked at. Don't try to be a tough guy when it comes to your vision." Dave looked around and called for a paramedic.

Jay was brought out to an ambulance where his eye was washed out and evaluated by an EMT. The irritation in his eye, although totally annoying, was paled by the emotions of the bloodbath.

29

The attendance at the funeral was impressive. In addition to four busloads from AllSport, the church was filled to capacity with Bob's family, friends, and associates. In spite of his tremendous grief at the loss of his best friend, Reid, at the request of Karen Thomas, gave a heartfelt eulogy. Tears as well as laughs filled the church as Reid told stories about his friend.

• • •

Days later, with a patch on his eye, Jay Scott was on stage at AllSport's theater, directing a meeting. In attendance was everyone who had worked on the case, including Jay's entire team as well as Dave Wheeler's. In the front row, next to Reid and Buck, were Karen Thomas and Reid's wife Shane. Jay had tried to convince Karen not to attend but she had insisted. He knew that some of the things he was going to say would cause her pain.

"Folks, I called this meeting so I could give you answers to some of the questions you may have about the case. Let me begin by thanking you all for your help. I hope you have been able to get a little rest and catch up with your families." He glanced toward Karen with a sympathetic look. She acknowledged with slight nod.

He continued, "This case led us in so many directions that it took a huge team to follow up on all the leads. We covered four countries on this one.

"We found out some interesting things during our interviews in the hospital. We also continued to review recorded phone calls between Joe Spinelli and Bob as well as some between Joe and the gang members he hired for the hit.

"Joe had been diverting funds for quite a while. We have retrieved over two million so far from three accounts, and we believe there is at least another million to come.

"Although Bob made a mistake in not immediately reporting the situation to Reid and Buck, his intentions were good. After he confronted Joe with his knowledge of the theft, Joe made him an offer to split the money. Bob not only vehemently turned him down, but became enraged that Joe would even contemplate making the offer. He told Joe that he was deciding how he could make sure that his time in jail would be kept to a minimum. But warned him that if he even mentioned paying him off again, he would make sure Joe would face the maximum penalty for his crime.

"I'm pretty sure that makes some of you feel better. I know it did for me. I was having a hard time understanding why Bob had not turned Joe in immediately."

Many heads in the audience nodded.

"Now I'll give you a quick explanation of how Joe came to hire the gang for the hit and how things turned against him in the end.

"Once Joe knew that Bob had caught him and couldn't be bribed, he made the decision to have Bob killed. He contacted Joe Morgan in jail. For those of you who don't know who Morgan is, he's the gang member who had sent Reid death threats, and then placed a hit on him a few years ago.

"Spinelli correctly figured that stewing in jail would create a strong desire for vengeance. We convinced Morgan to talk to us.

He informed us that Spinelli had contacted him, anonymously of course, with a plan for revenge against Reid. Spinelli had offered him ten grand for the name and number of someone who would be willing to kill Reid's best friend for cash. Morgan only discovered Spinelli's identity after the airport massacre." Jay took a sip of water from his glass on the podium.

"Anyway, we were able to pull information from the one gang member who survived. Spinelli set up the hit, then took off on his trip to Nepal. He had given the gang instructions to call his cell after the hit for information about where to pick up the final payment. He left a message on a cell phone that he purchased just for this reason. It seems that when they called the number, the message never played; hence they thought Spinelli stiffed them.

"It gets even more convoluted. The gang got greedy and changed their plans. Before the hit, they decided to extort more money from Spinelli. They left him a message saying that he would have to pay an additional fifty thousand. If he didn't agree to it, they would dump Bob's body where it would be found instead of disposing of it, as originally agreed. If he didn't pay after that, they would give the police an anonymous tip explaining Spinelli's involvement in the murder.

"Spinelli had already made the mistake of thinking that once his plan was in place he could just get out of town until it was all over. It seems trusting a gang is not too smart." Jay's face contorted with sarcasm.

"Well, the mistake was very costly to Joe. As you know, the gang dumped the body right here at AllSport. When they couldn't collect the second payment, they decided to take him out at the airport. You all know the result of that decision.

More nods from the audience.

"For those of you who don't know it, Spinelli is out of intensive care and it looks like he will live a long, unhappy life where he belongs, behind bars. Now, before we adjourn this meeting, I know Reid and Buck would like to say a few words."

Reid and Buck climbed the stairs and walked to the podium. Buck gestured for Reid to take the microphone.

"Folks, I'm going to make this quick. I want to thank you all on behalf of Bob's wife, Karen, as well as Buck and myself. This has been a very painful week for us, and you have helped us bring closure to Bob's untimely death. The recovery of the money seems unimportant in comparison to catching those responsible for his murder. I know many of you spent countless hours without sleep or seeing your families during the investigation. I want to express my gratitude to you all. My wife Shane is handing out envelopes to each of you. A portion of the enclosed money is the reward that was going to be offered by AllSport and the ICSF. Buck and I added to it to show our appreciation for your efforts. Officers, I know it is against department regulations to accept money for doing your job, but I have received clearance for this."

Most of the officers looked at Wheeler, who nodded and showed them *his* envelope as he placed it in an inside pocket of his sport coat.

"All I ask is that you use some of the money to take your families on vacation. Have some fun; you all deserve it." He paused and the audience started to applaud.

He held up his hand to quiet them. "One more thing before we let you go. Those of you who were lucky enough to know Bob, probably knew that he was a basketball fanatic. It struck me as ludicrous that he was found just outside the basketball dome. Well, I would like you all to attend a ceremony next week, where we will be dedicating the dome to Bob. It will be called the Bob Thomas Basketball Arena and there will be a room inside that will be a tribute to him. On one wall will be plaques with each of your names inscribed on them."

The room filled with nods, smiles, and quiet conversation.

"Folks, I'm almost done. Some of you may know that once a year a group of AllSport's biggest contributors enjoy a weekend of fun, food, and sport here on campus. Buck and I have decided to add another weekend of fun to the schedule. It will be the Bob Thomas Memorial Weekend. You will all receive invitations for you and your families to come and celebrate Bob's life. It will not be a weekend of mourning; Bob wouldn't have liked that. It will be a weekend of sports, both recreational and competitive, with some of the best pros in the country on hand to help train and compete with you and your kids. We will house you in our guest housing and there will be plenty of food. I really don't know a better way to show respect for my dear friend and I want you all to take part. Thank you all."

He finished to another round of applause. As he walked down the steps Karen approached with a tear-soaked smile. She hugged Reid.

"Thank you for this, he would have loved it," she said between sobs.

"I think you're right, Karen, I certainly hope so."